I0520481

HUNTER

BRAWLERS

J.M. DABNEY

Copyright © 2018 J.M. Dabney
Cover Art: Reese Dante (reesedante.com)
Editor: Laura McNellis

All rights reserved. Printed in the United States of America. No part of this book may be used or reproduced in any manner whatsoever without written permission except in the case of brief quotations in critical articles or reviews.

This book is a work of fiction. Names, characters, businesses, organizations, places, events and incidents either are the product of the author's imagination or are used fictitiously. Any resemblance to actual persons, living or dead, events, or locales is entirely coincidental.

Cover content is for illustrative purposes only. Any person depicted on the cover is a model.

ISBN-13: 978-1-947184-14-5

DEDICATION

To the ones who wanted to meet the Brawlers.

CONTENTS

1 DID YOU JUST TRIP OVER AIR?

Hunter Black opened his calendar app and inputted his accident list of the day. His large hands quickly tapped the screen.

Accident 1: Stabbed himself with a corkscrew

Accident 2: Squirted lemon juice into my eye.

Accident 3: Possible concussion from tripping over air.

Fourth and Final: I walked into a brass knuckle enforced punch thrown by his coworker Psycho.

He was a fuck up, he knew it, and everyone else did too. He straddled his bike in the empty parking lot of Brawlers Bar where he worked. All he wanted was one damn day where he didn't attempt to kill himself. From the moment he took his first step it was downhill from there. By the time he was five, his medical record was an inch thick. Burns, broken bones, accidents big and small. Inside the manila folder didn't always give the truth. Not all his wounds were accidents. His parents loathed the odd child they had been cursed with, and they showed him just how unwanted he was.

All he had wanted was their love. Instead, he received pain and fear. When his I.Q. was tested, he had become more of an oddity. At sixteen, he'd graduated from high school and headed to college, homeless.

He turned his phone off and slipped it into his jacket pocket. Hunter raised his hands and slipped his reading glasses off. He didn't want to remember, that wasn't this life anymore, and he had new family and friends. A home he wouldn't have to worry about losing. Warm and never hungry. He shook his head and glanced around the parking lot.

Scary and Tank's bikes were still parked in their reserved spots, their husband Elijah was inside with them. Everyone else already left for the night. He picked up his helmet where it was balanced between his thighs and lifted it to pull it on.

The Sheriff's cruiser was still parked across the street. Local law enforcement loved to give them shit, but he'd noticed the same deputy assigned every weekend for at least the last year. Crave said the guy seemed cool and didn't give them shit, the only people he'd pulled over were visibly drunk when they started their vehicles. He closed the visor and started his bike, he pulled out slowly and headed toward home.

He slowed even more as he passed the deputy. The interior of the car was dark so he couldn't see what the guy looked like. He didn't know why he cared. He had another two years of probation, he didn't need to be fucking with cops—even friendly ones. Once he was far enough away, he accelerated, and the deep growl of his engine brought a smile to his face.

It was the one place he felt free. He wasn't Hunter Black the fuck up ex-con. When he'd been sixteen, a crew approached him. It was a simple hack job. They just needed a few alarm systems deactivated. He could do that shit in his sleep. The money was easy, and he never went inside, just shut down the systems, and the crew took care of the rest. Except for the last job that went from bad to worse.

First degree Grand Theft charge on his eighteenth birthday. He'd taken one step into the building, one, Hunter hadn't touched anything, and nothing was found on him except his laptop and phone. None of that mattered when the crew removed almost two hundred thousand in diamonds from a safe.

It was an old fucking cliché, eighteen and in his third year of college. Kid from a bad neighborhood making good, but his scholarship only went so far, and he had to live. The full academic ride didn't pay for a place to live or food. He fucked up like he always had and he'd paid for it with five years and another five years' probation.

He liked the Brawlers Crew. He had a nice room and a job that paid well. Hunter wanted more, but what that was he didn't know.

His headlight hit a set of eyes in the middle of the road, so he swerved to avoid hitting whatever it was. Which he learned was a mistake as flashing lights, and a siren rose above the sound of his engine.

Shit, his stomach had started twisting as he slowly pulled to the side. He kicked down the stand and removed his helmet. *Just stay cool, Hunter, just explain*—holy fuck, he turned his upper body almost completely around as he'd caught sight of the deputy. His compact body shown off in the uniform. The shirt strained across a broad muscled chest, and the short sleeves barely contained the mass of large biceps.

He must live in a gym. Hunter was big but genetics attributed to that, and he also sported a bit of a belly. His arms were covered in hair, but the deputy's skin was smooth. The few men he'd hooked up with since his release complained about his hairy body. Why the fuck was he thinking about that? He was probably getting ready to be arrested.

"Sir, do you know why I pulled you over," the deputy's voice a soothing baritone.

Really, was that in the handbook to ask at every traffic stop? *Don't say it, Hunter,* he ordered himself.

"I swerved." He kept his answer short and to the point. If he learned one thing over his life, it was to keep his mouth shut around anyone with a badge.

"And why did you swerve?"

"My headlight caught on eyes in the middle of the road. I tried to avoid it."

"Have you been drinking tonight, sir?"

"No, I was working, and I don't drink."

The deputy stepped closer and strong, broad features came into view. If not for the beard the guy looked young, maybe a few years older than his twenty-six.

"Can I see your license and registration?"

"Sure, I gotta reach into my backpack."

"Go ahead."

He tensed as he noticed the subtle move of the deputy repositioning his left hand on his sidearm.

Hunter swung his pack off his shoulders and pulled it around to his lap. He opened the zipper and reached inside for his wallet. He took out the cards and handed them to the deputy. The man used the flashlight to check the information.

"Mr. Black, I'm going to let you go, but be careful. These back roads aren't exactly safe this late."

He was surprised the deputy didn't call it in, but he wasn't going to complain. The man would look closer at him if the deputy knew his background.

"Thank you." He reached out to take his cards back and slid them back into his wallet then his bag. Hunter zipped it and slipped his arms back into the straps.

"Have a good night, Mr. Black."

"You too, be safe." He didn't know what made him say it, but it was already out, and he restarted his bike.

Hunter took off, speeding up to the limit and hoped to get home without another stop. Next time by a cop who wasn't as friendly as the one he'd just pulled away from.

It was only another ten minutes before he pulled into the yard of the farmhouse. The porch light was still on, and he noticed a few lights burned dimly. Bull was probably just curling up with his husband, Gregory. Crave and Twitch would be trying to break their bed as they did every night. At least Psycho didn't live in the house anymore. He was getting damned tired of listening to everyone get laid but him.

He didn't want to think about how long since he'd been in a man's bed. It wasn't like he hadn't tried. He'd even gone out on a few dates, but with his friends, background and jobs, it didn't work out.

He parked and dismounted. Hunter stood back staring up at the house. Maybe he should just crash in the barn since it was quieter, and he wouldn't get jealous of the happy couples.

He quietly jogged up to the porch and then inside, locking the door behind him. No one was around, but he heard Crave trying to make Twitch break glass with his screams. Bull and Gregory weren't far behind.

He pulled his earbuds from his pocket and shoved them into his ears, then started his music as loud as he could stand. Hunter headed to his room at the back of the house. He closed the door and locked it.

Carefully, Hunter set his bag on his desk and started to strip, he walked toward the bathroom to wash off the scents of stale beer and alcohol. The night couldn't be over fast enough. In the bathroom, he removed his earbuds, then the last of his clothes and looked into the mirror.

Hunter pinched his love handles, then cupped his stomach giving it a little shake. He didn't have an issue with his body, but he hadn't really found anyone who liked it. Thoughts of the gorgeous deputy filled his head, and he groaned. Not going there, he spun away from the mirror. He quickly started the shower and stepped beneath the slowly warming spray.

"Tomorrow will be a better day," he repeated in a whisper and didn't believe a damn word he said.

2 STUPID MOVE, WREN

Deputy Wren Gramble clenched his hands around the steering wheel of his *Jeep* until his knuckles turned white. He'd signed out ten minutes ago and was headed home to his apartment across town. Two years there or not, being the new guy sucked, he always got the shit assignments and shifts. Although he couldn't complain too much about staking out a gay bar in the middle of nowhere. The scenery was damn nice.

Everyone complained, and the barely veiled homophobic comments couldn't be missed. It wasn't everyone, and he liked some of the guys he worked with, but sometimes he wanted to knock the fuck out of them. He'd already been transferred from his last job for his problem with authority. Power was the end of the line. Eight years in law enforcement and he was about to have to look for a new line of work.

He pulled off in front of a diner deciding he wanted breakfast before he crawled into bed. Several motorcycles were lined up outside. He recognized one of them, the sexy Hunter Black. The man he'd pulled over in the wee hours of the morning. Okay, he'd been a bit of a stalker the last six months. He'd noticed him one night, Hunter the last one to leave and had set on his bike tapping out some message on his phone. The man was frowning, and he'd wanted to rid the man of the sadness—he didn't know why he found the man so irresistible.

Wren got out of his vehicle and jogged up to the door and pulled it open. He was in a hurry to catch sight of Hunter during the day. He had only ever seen Hunter in the shadows.

"Dude, I didn't piss him off." A big man with dark skin scowled. "It's your fault he won't feed us."

"I didn't mean to drop his cake." The familiar voice whined, and he caught sight of Hunter sitting at a table with familiar faces, they were all employees he'd seen at Brawlers.

"You never mean…" A huge blond he recognized as the guy who worked the door shook his head and tore into an overflowing plate of food. "My man wouldn't even cook for me."

"You could fuck up breathing." A massive graying man scowled.

Wren growled at them ganging up on Hunter. The man's head was lowered, and his long hair shielded his face as he picked at his own breakfast.

"This is loving on my husband time and what am I doing? Sitting here with you bastards," the blond huffed.

"I think Twitch's ass could use a break. What would this be round three for the day," Hunter asked.

Wren almost laughed as he took a seat at the counter closest to their table.

"You have seen my husband, right?"

"Didn't you tell me you'd burn out my eyes with Bull's welding torch if I looked at him," Hunter asked.

"True." a brutal smirk tilted the blond's mouth proved he'd go through with it.

Wren had witnessed the viciousness of these men over the few years he'd been assigned to watch the bar. They didn't take any prisoners.

"How Twitch puts up with you amazes me," the dark-skinned man quipped with a snort.

"My boy loves everything I do to him."

"Yeah, we've heard enough of it over the last year and a half. Gregory's stocked the nightstand with a year's supply of earplugs."

"Hey, I don't want to hear it, you two ain't any better. I hear him yell Daddy one more fucking time, I'm going to shove screwdrivers into my ears to bust my eardrums. That's fucking disturbing."

"Hey, Wren, what can I get ya?" Heidi, the normal morning waitress, asked him with a smile.

"Coffee and my usual please."

"Sure, honey, ignore that crew, they're pissed Twitch is refusing to cook for them."

"Twitch?"

A picture of a short brunet man who leaned a bit toward the androgynous side flashed in his head. Beautiful and delicate, and he always saw the man plastered to the blond's side.

"Crave's husband. Hunter dropped a cake that Twitch was making as a sort of audition for a part time job for Ben, Psycho's husband, at the man's bakery."

She talked about husbands like it wasn't a big thing. He tended to forget that the good people in town outnumbered the bigots. It was one of the reasons he'd started to love living there.

Her smile was filled with fondness as she glanced at the table filled with the huge, mean looking men.

"They're like big babies." She raised her voice.

"Hey," four gruff voices said in unison.

"Don't hey me, at least once a week y'all are up in here bitching about those men of yours. You just better be grateful y'all got men."

He turned to glance over his shoulder to find Hunter watching him. Eyes so pale blue you could barely distinguish between the whites and the irises stared into his. His smile turned to a frown as the man looked away finding his almost full plate fascinating.

"You're the new deputy, right," Crave asked.

"Not so new, been around a few years." He stood to turn and extend his hand.

"Huh, didn't think you were stuck on Brawler duty that long."

"I've been posted out at Brawlers about the last year."

He shook each man's hand as they introduced themselves, except for Hunter who didn't reach out to shake. Hunter almost seemed to be avoiding touching him. He didn't understand why that hurt as much as it did. It wasn't like he knew Hunter, but he kind of wanted the man to like him.

"Thanks for not being a dick like the rest. They take every opportunity to bust our balls." Psycho finished his plate and pushed it away.

"It's not a bad gig. Boring most nights."

"Join us." Bull's voice held authority.

"I don't want to intrude."

"Sit your ass down unless you don't want to be associated," Bull asked with a raised, thick gray brow.

Wren took the seat Psycho kicked out, and Heidi set his coffee and plate in front of him. He realized instead of at the end of the table Psycho chose the one right next to Hunter. He looked at Psycho to find the man smiling at him. Not really smiling, it was more of a grimace, but probably as good as it got. The man didn't have laugh lines beside his dark eyes.

"Eavesdropping on the pathetic married men, Deputy," Psycho asked.

"Y'all ain't the quietest bunch."

"Can't deny that, except for our Hunter here. Not much of a talker." Bull smiled at the man.

These men gave each other shit as a pastime activity. He still didn't like Hunter being the focus of it though. Wren was being stupid. Clearly, the man wasn't interested.

"Why haven't you come in for a drink yet? You probably get the shit hours, but they can't work you seven days a week?" Bull waved at Heidi to get her attention.

"I'll be right there, everyone need a refill?"

"Yes, ma'am."

Wren started eating as the conversation continued around him. Did these people not know what polite conversation was or inside voices? He nearly choked on his food several times.

"Best not to eat when this crew or the Twirled one are together," A soft, slightly raspy voice came from his right.

He turned his head to see Hunter smiling at him through a curtain of dark hair. Wren glanced at Hunter's plate to see it untouched.

"I learned my lesson when I nearly choked to death," Hunter's voice was serious.

"That bad huh?"

"Sometimes."

"Do you want to move to another table?"

"Why?"

"I don't know, maybe talk?"

"Okay."

The guy was nervous as hell, and he didn't know why. Hunter stood and slung the strap of his backpack over his shoulder, then picked up his plate and mug. Wren grabbed his own and followed Hunter to a table in the far corner. Hunter's steps were slow and careful, then even slower until he set everything down.

"You seem a bit shy or is it just me," Wren asked with a smile.

"You."

The blunt answer took Wren by surprise.

"Don't like cops?"

"Not exactly fans of me or the crew."

"True, they seem to think y'all are pains in the ass."

"Among other things."

"Do you work every night?"

"No, my usual days off are Wednesday and Thursday, weekends are all hands-on deck."

"Want to get dinner maybe Wednesday?"

He didn't know where the offer of a date came from, but he didn't regret it.

"Really?"

"Yeah."

"Okay, where do you want to meet? Somewhere out of town?"

"No, give me your phone." Wren held out his hand, and after unlocking it, Hunter handed it over. "I'm going to put my number in, and you can call me later, then we can decide when I should pick you up."

He entered his info and saved it, he called his own phone so he'd have Hunter's number just in case the shy man had second thoughts. Which if the nervous shifting of his food around the plate and the quick peeks were any indication, he was in for a challenge. Good damn thing he was stubborn.

"Finish eating, Hunter."

Hunter nodded and started eating. Wren slid the phone across the table and took the opportunity to study the man. To be honest, he'd pulled the man over on purpose that morning. He could've found some excuse, but Hunter swerving gave him the perfect one. It was a stupid move, now Hunter feared him.

Maybe a date without him in uniform would ease Hunter's fears. Wren hoped because he sure as hell was getting some time alone with the handsome and quiet Hunter.

"Matty, I said no, don't even think about it," A deep, frustrated voice drew Wren's attention.

He turned his head to look back over his shoulder to find a muscular man trailing after the cutest little redhead. The kid's chunky legs moving faster than his upper body. The kid, Matty, made grabby hands and headed straight for Heidi. She held out a cookie.

"Heidi, don't fucking think…shit." The stranger dropped his broad, scruffy jaw to his chest and sighed. "You know he's spending the night with me, right?"

"Yes, Priest was in earlier, and gave me all the information on Lucky and his romantic plans."

"So, you just had to give the little former parasite sugar?"

"You know it."

"Why do you hate me," the masculine man whined.

"I don't hate you, you're one of my biggest customers. Speaking of that, what do you need?"

"I just need a coffee to go, Matty and I will be back for dinner. Right now, I was going to take him to the office with me so I could finish this week's security assignments."

"Buck up, Linus, it's not that bad. A little sugar never hurt anybody."

"Um, have we forgotten a certain pretty brunet?"

"Don't call my husband pretty," Crave yelled.

"Ease up, Crave, you know that man doesn't have eyes for anyone but you. As much as I hate to quote my brother, you didn't have to Golden Shower…"

Wren snorted, and narrowed eyes turned toward him.

"Matty, come here, don't make me get the leash."

Wren swore the little boy rolled his eyes.

Linus turned toward him and started for the table, while Matty headed in the opposite direction. Wren didn't look away until Matty had crawled into Bull's lap and leaned back, gnawed on his cookie.

"Hey, Hunter, new friend," Linus asked suspiciously.

"Hi, Linus, this is Wren, Wren, this is Lucky's—"

Linus grunted.

"Lucky's not that bad."

"Says the gorgeous man who didn't grow up with him."

Wren darted his gaze between them, he didn't miss the interest in Linus' eyes.

"I'm not…"

"Shut up, what's the rule?"

Hunter rolled his eyes. "The Trentons, unfortunately, can't tell a lie, so shut up and take a fucking compliment."

"Exactly."

Strange eyes that were an odd swirling of bright blue and a dark forest green met his, and he suddenly wanted to shift uncomfortably in his seat.

"Linus, you're the newest criminal of the Powers Sheriff Department," The man, Linus, said.

"I think the title is Deputy."

"Naw, corruption runs deep among the criminals behind their badges."

"Not a fan of law enforcement?"

"Don't let him fool you, Wren, he used to wear a badge."

"Briefly, before I realized I'm not much on rules, and Internal Affairs liked to bust my balls."

"Substantiated claims?"

"Not really, they didn't like the company I kept, in particular, my mother."

"Lily is just a free spirit."

"She's a menace."

Hunter chuckled, and Wren turned to take in his bright, humor-filled eyes. Okay, he thought he's feeling jealousy for the first time. Which was stupid, these men seemed to be friends, maybe just friends on Hunter's side but not Linus'.

"What's your latest blanket?"

"Tits."

Hunter barked out a loud laugh.

Wren stared at Linus. He was lost in the face of an apparent inside joke.

"He doesn't get the reference, care to enlighten him, Hunter?"

"Linus plus blankets equals…"

"Oh shit, no."

Who the hell would do that to their child? It opened the kid up to a lifetime of jokes.

"My parents and siblings take great pleasure in my birthday and Christmas blankets, each one more inappropriate than the last."

"The less risqué ones he passes out to the homeless every year."

"What about the risqué ones?"

"Hunter gets them."

"Why?"

"He's always cold at night."

The man said it like Wren was a moron.

"I don't want the tits one."

"Didn't think you would, it's in my guest room closet with the rest of the ones you wouldn't take."

"If you don't want them, why don't you throw them away?"

"My family is all shades of fucked up, but they're family. Hunter," Linus' voice carried an odd tone.

"No."

"Come on, baby, my mother loves you. Don't make me say please."

"Oh, I know how painful to your blackened soul politeness is but the answer is still no. Last camping trip, I don't know how I ended up sandwiched between Damon and Lily."

"You were shivering."

"No excuses, your dad poking me was very…awkward."

"Fine, make me spend three days in the middle of bumfuck nowhere with the screamers while we commune with nature and align our Chakras and chant."

"You'll have fun."

"Whatever you say, now, have you seen Trouble?"

"Give it to me."

He watched as Hunter held out his hand and a small black bag was placed on his palm.

"You got the pliers?"

"Yep."

Wren narrowed his eyes as he took in the scene in front of him.

"If you'd leave the damn things in…"

Linus cut Crave off with an absently thrown middle finger.

"If Matty starts doing that, I'm going to kick your—"

"Keep cussing, old man, see who gets in trouble first."

He slumped back in his chair as Linus sat down, his thick thighs bracketed Hunter's as the man fumbled with the bag.

"You sure you want me to do this?"

"Quit, you're fine. You're not a fuck up. You're just…clumsy."

Hunter sighed loudly, and Wren took it all in. Hunter carefully replaced eyebrow, lip, and septum rings. He didn't fail to notice Linus had his hands on Hunter's thighs and was stroking them with his thumbs. Hunter seemed calm and focused. Maybe dating Hunter wasn't such a good idea. It seemed he already had a man interested in him and they had history. Linus didn't have the badge that made Hunter so nervous.

"Wren asked me to dinner," Hunter spoke quietly.

"He did, you'll have fun."

Hunter might be oblivious, but he wasn't, Linus didn't like the mention of a date. The man was gorgeous and sexy, he had that asshole personality some men liked. It wasn't his thing, but he couldn't deny it turned him on a bit. He grimaced at the thought, he had only moments ago asked Hunter out, now he was checking out the man who appeared to be his competition.

"All done. Now, leave them in."

"I got an operation in a couple of days, so I needed to blend, after that they're gone."

"Only to have to hunt someone down to put them back in the next time. Vest."

"It was a flesh wound, you made too much of a deal about it."

"Whatever."

"Yeah, whatever. I got to get moving. A new client needs twenty-four seven, and I'm short on bodies."

"Hire more people."

"I'll try."

"You always say you'll try and what happens?"

"Don't start, Hunter, we talked about this."

"I'm not fighting with you. I won't come to the hospital next time."

"You'll be there."

Hunter looked down at his lap, and his hair fell to conceal his face, Linus raised his hands and tucked it behind the man's ears. Linus bent until the man could stare into Hunter's eyes.

"Don't worry so much. Have fun, don't worry about tomorrow, okay?"

Firm, full lips brushed Hunter's forehead. The caress innocent enough in appearance, but there was also an intimacy to it. A familiarity and he wondered how many times Linus kissed Hunter—touched him. He shook his head and pushed the thoughts away. The only thing they brought him was a sense of hesitancy that hadn't been there before Linus walked through the door of the diner.

"Okay."

One minute, Linus was there and the next he was gone. Did Hunter not see that Linus was head over heels for him?

Hunter turned back to the table and picked at his food.

"I better get going myself."

"Okay."

"I'll call you about that date or text me with a time you're free."

"It was nice seeing you again, Wren."

"You too."

He didn't know why he was being so short with the man, he wanted Hunter, but it looked like someone else did too. He was too tired to analyze it. If Hunter called, he called. He said his goodbyes and paid his check. He headed toward the exit without looking back. Why did it feel like he was walking away from the one person he'd been searching for?

3 HOW THE FUCK DID SOMEONE DATE?

Wren: *Say yes.*

Hunter read the text from Wren for the twentieth time since he'd awakened. He was being an idiot and kept putting off meeting Wren for dinner. It wasn't like he didn't want to. The man was beyond gorgeous, and Hunter didn't understand why Wren insisted so strongly on them going out.

He shoved his hands through his hair and winced as his fingers caught in a few tangles. How much longer could he keep putting it off before the man gave up? Hunter didn't want that. He looked at his reflection in the bar's bathroom mirror and gingerly pushed at the swollen, bruised bump on his cheekbone.

Rarely did he lose his temper, but Crave got on his last nerve. Just as his fist almost connected with the arrogant bastard's jaw Bull blocked it with his forearm. That one loss of control ended with him in the ring. Rules at

Brawlers Farm were clear, no fighting outside the ring and his carelessly thrown punch equated to a thrown gauntlet.

His injuries could've been worse than a black eye, a small cut over his eye and a busted lip. His ribs hurt like a fucker, but he knew Crave pulled most of his punches. Over the few years of living and working with the Brawler Crew, he'd seen them practically take each other's heads off.

Hunter couldn't go out with Wren looking like that. He was tired and sore, and he just wanted to go home.

He turned and headed for the door, when he opened it he found Twitch leaned back against the opposite wall.

"So, wanna talk about it?"

"No."

"Too damn bad. What has your manties in a bunch?"

He sighed and leaned his shoulder and the side of his head to the frame, "Someone asked me out."

"Customer?"

"No, you don't buy your meat where you make your bread, man."

"Good, because we got enough drama around here. Is it that deputy the guys were telling me about? Crave said he asked you to sit with him and talk."

"Fuck, Twitch, he's gorgeous and I ain't just saying that. He's broad and compact with these bulging muscles. I don't see how his uniform contains it all."

"That good huh?"

He sighed. "You got no fucking idea."

"So, what's the problem? You ain't got laid in forever."

"Don't remind me." He crossed his arms over his chest. "He asked me to have dinner, maybe it's not even a date."

"From what the crew said, the man definitely had a date in mind among other things. So, I'm still not seeing the issue."

"Look at me."

"I see you every damn day."

"Quit being obtuse. I did say the man is gorgeous, right? I'm like the fucking chunky missing link. So hairy I'm like a loofah. I doubt the man wants to be exfoliated while he fucks someone. Just what someone wants to hear afterward, thanks for the rug burn."

Would his shame not end?

Twitch laughed so hard he snorted and covered his mouth.

"Oh my fuck, I'm so sorry," Twitch apologized even as he bent at the waist to laugh louder. "I can't fucking breathe."

"I hate you." Hunter stomped down the hall with Twitch on his heels. "I don't like your husband," he yelled as he reached over the bar to grab his backpack.

"What the fuck is going on," Crave bellowed.

"Exfoliate," Twitch wheezed, "Loofah. Rugburn."

"Are you two high," Crave asked and shook his head.

"I'm going home."

"Tell me what the fuck you did before you leave. Did you give him sugar," Crave asked as he followed Hunter.

He tried to ignore them, he really did, and busted through the front exit. Crave grabbed his arm to spin him around.

"What the fuck is going on here," Wren's pissed voice boomed in the night.

"Just fucking great," Hunter muttered under his breath.

"I got that." Crave pointed over his shoulder to a giggling Twitch. "Did you give him sugar? You know what happens," Crave yelled.

"I didn't give him sugar."

Twitch moaned obscenely, "Oh yeah, yes, yes," then he screamed, "rug burn."

"I will make Crave a fucking widower, you little shit," Hunter threatened.

He started to move around Crave only to find him blocked by a wide hand on his chest. Just great, fingers tangled in his chest hair where the loose v-neckline dipped.

"Everyone calm the hell…" Wren suddenly turned on him, and his eyes narrowed. "What the fuck happened to your face?"

"It's nothing."

"It's not nothing, did you go to the ER?"

"Twitch stitched him up, no big deal. He should learn to block or at least fucking duck. I mean damn I've kicked his ass—"

"You fucking did that?" Wren spun to face Crave.

Things were getting out of hand quick.

"Yeah, he threw a punch, Bull made us take it to the ring."

"What the fuck are you talking about?"

Hunter reached out and grabbed Wren's tight, trim waist. The man was solid muscle with not even the slightest give under his hands. Not a chance in hell he was going out with this man. He'd never fucking get naked in front of him.

He leaned down to whisper in Wren's ear, "Wren, it's okay. Let Crave go take care of Twitch before he pisses himself. I'll explain." He tugged the man backward and away from Crave.

Crave was notorious for finishing a fight and Twitch would kill Hunter if his man landed himself in jail. The last time Crave came out beat to hell and not talking about what happened. It was well-known the cops around there didn't care for the Brawler Crew. For a town with a visible LGBT population, the authorities were bigoted as fuck.

"You better explain quick before I—"

"There's a lot of testosterone out at the farm. Sometimes shit gets out of hand. Bull made a rule when he started taking in the strays who worked at Brawlers. If we were going to fight, then we'd take it to the ring he had built in the barn. No bare knuckles or intentional injuries. Also, when we leave the ring, our anger stays inside."

"And you got in the ring."

"Crave was being an asshole, and I swung without thinking. And per Bull's rules that meant a few rounds on the mat."

"But, baby, look at your face."

Wren raised his hands to stroke the calloused tips of his face gently. He almost jerked away at the contact. Hunter liked the man's touch too much and since nothing was going to happen there was no way in hell he was going to have memories to torture himself with later.

"It's fine. Crave took it easy on me. Pulled most of his punches which is weird for him, but I ain't a brawler."

"You haven't agreed to our date yet?"

"A date, I just thought—"

"No, you didn't, you knew I wanted a date, and you're putting it off, why?"

"If you knew my past you wouldn't want to date me."

That was the part he didn't want to admit. The Brawlers knew, but only his bosses and Bull knew the whole story. All the rest knew was he was a computer nerd who went to prison for hacking.

"And why do you say that?"

He dropped his stare to the ground. He didn't want to look at Wren when he said it because he didn't want to see the disappointment or goodbye in his eyes.

"I got out of prison two years ago, I got another three years of probation."

Wren didn't pull back, just placed his hands beneath Hunter's chin and lifted his gaze. "What did you do?"

"I hacked a few security systems. Last job went nuclear, and someone fucked up."

"Why did you do it?"

"I needed to pay some shit for school, and the money was easy. I was eighteen but got recruited two years earlier. It was nice not to struggle or live in my car. I could eat whenever I was hungry. Slept someplace warm every night."

"I'm not going to say I'm not surprised or whatever. There's no excuse for it, not even your age, but I don't have the whole story. That being said, why don't you tell me about it over dinner tomorrow night?"

"Really?"

"Yeah, really, I can come out to the farm and pick you up."

"You sure you want to be seen in public with me, the department you work for isn't—"

"Let me handle that, so, what's it going to be? Keep putting it off or actually go out with me like you want to?"

"Who said I wanted to?"

Wren just shook his head and stepped back. "I have to get back to work. Behave and no more time in the ring. I don't like it."

"I don't take—"

"Yes, you do, and you'll like it. Get home, I'll see you at six and be ready."

Wren got back in his car and slammed the door before he had a chance to respond.

"Do you think that's a good idea," Crave asked from behind him.

"Not in the fucking least."

"Finally, something we agree on."

He sensed when he was finally alone, and he watched the last of the running lights from Wren's vehicle fade in the distance. Hunter had a bad feeling this was going to be his worse fuck up yet.

4 WAS WREN GOING TO HAVE TO FIGHT FOR HIS LIFE TO PICK HUNTER UP?

Wren pulled up to a huge, two-story farmhouse. Motorcycles were lined up in front of a white picket fence. A beat-up truck was parked between a barn and a smaller building. Where it should be peaceful, it was absolute chaos.

"Goddammit, Crave, turn down the fucking music. It ain't drowning out Twitch's glass-shattering squeals," a pissed off familiar voice bellowed from the house.

Wren could hear it where he was parked a good distance from the house. Yelling blended with obvious sex sounds from a downstairs window.

"Prep him next time," the same voice was punctuated with a slamming door.

"Hunter, are you ready, it's almost six," a calmer voice broke through the pandemonium.

A loud cry echoed in the early evening, and he instantly went on alert. He spun on his heels toward the trees to find a massive man he recognized as Psycho with a smaller man bent over the railing of a nearby cottage.

Wren was about to get in the car and make a run for it. What had he gotten himself into?

"Hunter, sweetie, you're gonna be late, save your work and get moving."

"Almost done, dammit, give me a minute."

"Clean up your lube. Twitch almost broke his neck the last time he cleaned your room—"

"I'm not jerking off, I have some fucking restraint, unlike your husband—"

"Leave Bull out of this. Archer, our son is mouthing off."

His lips started to twitch.

"You adopted his hairy ass, Gregory, I said no."

"Shit, we got an audience," the calmer one, Gregory, yelled, and seconds later, the door flew open. "Don't run," the man warned.

Wren froze waiting for some kind of attack. A downstairs window opened all the way and two naked men, one of them Crave, leaned out of it. Both flushed and looking toward the porch.

"What the fuck is going on, we under attack?" Crave demanded.

"Get back inside, shit," Gregory power walked off the porch.

"Don't get your manties in a bunch, pop."

"I didn't adopt your ass, so get back inside. I'm surprised Hunter's date is still here. Hi," Gregory waved.

"Hey, Wren," Crave said with a smirk and then dragged the tiny man back into the house.

He didn't even have time to respond before a high-pitched squeal behind him broke the temporary silence.

"Psycho, take your man inside," Gregory admonished. "I'm so sorry, we're normally better than this. I'm Gregory, Bull's mine."

"Wren." He extended his hand, and the beautiful man shook it.

Gregory wasn't what he'd pictured the older, graying man's husband to look like. Gregory screamed designer tastes from the top of his perfectly styled hair to his expensive dress shoes.

"Gregory, our son is still naked, you're dealing with him."

"Quit embarrassing him, Bull, we've talked about this. Positive reinforcement."

"Baby, I'm positive he's still naked or Sasq—"

"Bull, get inside."

"Yes, dear," Bull grumbled.

"Come on inside, and I'll set you up with a drink or ten." Gregory turned away.

Wren swore the man mumbled, *I know I could use them.* Okay, this was beginning as the weirdest first date in history, and it hadn't even started yet.

"Is that what you're wearing?"

"Um, yes, is there—"

"Hunter, unlock your door, I need to see your closet," Gregory stomped away hollering.

The man was as bad as the rest of them. He stood just inside the door and looked around at the spotless living room.

"Don't look so fucking nervous." Bull peeked out of the kitchen. "Is my husband gone?"

"I think he wanted to see—"

"I heard. Hunter's going to be so bitchy. Come on, coffee or something stronger?"

"Stronger, but I'm driving so coffee would be great."

Wren strode toward the doorway Bull disappeared into and walked into a large kitchen. The kitchen smelled amazing. He didn't know what was cooking, but his stomach growled.

"Okay, ground rules." Bull turned to him with his arms crossed over his massive chest.

"I didn't think—"

"Shut up, Hunter can't be around sharp objects, no ladders, anything over two feet avoid it. No fire. He should have his insurance cards with him just in case..." Bull took a breath. "He's allergic to strawberries, peanuts, and dairy. He has an epi-pen. Don't make him eat anything green, not happening, you'll never get through dinner."

"Does he have a bedtime?"

He realized his mistake when Bull advanced and stood inches from him. Bull's nostrils flared, and his mismatched eyes glittered with anger.

"Be a smart ass on your own time, my husband loves Hunter likes his own, so if anything happens to him I gotta hear it. Hunter goes out of his way to be invisible. He'll pretend to be okay even when his throat's closing from an allergic reaction."

"Duly noted."

Bull backed up and retook his position leaned against the counter. "All our numbers are in his phone, two is speed dial for Gregory, and he'll be stalking his phone. I don't like this dating a cop bullshit, we get enough drama. But throw a gay ex-con Brawler employee on it, and you're setting Hunter up for retaliation. If anything happens to him, they won't find your body, got it?"

He was about to argue, but the menace in Bull's gaze stopped him. "Got it." Wren understood them being protective of Hunter. Seeing the bruises on Hunter's face last night brought out a protective streak he'd never had before.

"Gregory, quit fussing." Hunter's exasperated tone made him smile.

"It's your first date, I'm so nervous."

"It's my date, why are you nervous?"

"Because it's your first one ever and I want it to be great for you. I love you, remember," Gregory asked.

"I love you, too."

Hunter's response was so low Wren almost missed it. Gregory was probably only a decade older than Hunter, but there was a father/son relationship in play.

"You look so handsome, don't let them tell you different. Hold that chin up. You're worth some effort, remember that. You have condoms?"

"Gregory," Hunter said sharply.

Wren felt when Hunter walked into the room, and he turned with a smile. He froze as he took in Hunter. Damn, Hunter's hair was pulled back and braided letting him see the man's face without Hunter's usual camouflage. The masculine beauty of the softened angles of Hunter's face made him just want to stare.

"You're still here?" Hunter sounded shocked.

"Yeah, we had a date."

He almost felt guilty for his earlier inclination to run once he saw the nervousness that made Hunter fidget. The man had assumed he would run before he made it to the door. He knew Hunter was insecure and he didn't have a clue how to reassure him.

"I figured, ya know, you'd run."

"He seems like a nice young man, of course he wouldn't—"

"Bull, do something, please."

"I got'cha covered."

Wren turned just in time see a smirk tug at one corner of Bull's mouth, and the man stalked—and there was no other word for it—toward Gregory. The beautiful man seemed to melt as soon as Bull's arms came around him.

"Is it time for a bit of punishment, Daddy," Gregory whispered as he jumped and wrapped completely around Bull.

Wren raised a brow and watched at the heat building between the two men. Fuck, that was almost—

"You think ya deserve it, boy, ya might like it too much."

Gregory's slim body was slammed against the wall.

"Oh fuck, let's go."

Hunter had his hand wrapped around his wrist, and he was being hauled to the door like a pack of wild dogs were on their heels.

"They're so embarrassing, and they're considered the adults in the house."

"You did ask Bull to do something."

"Yeah, my mistake, I should have known. I'm sorry."

"No need, some people just have weird families. Let's get going, I'm starving."

He opened the passenger door of his *Jeep* and waited as Hunter considered it like it was a trap. This might be harder than he thought and he'd already figured out Hunter's strong resistance to dating him. He'd have to go slow, and that wasn't a big deal for him. He'd bed hopped for a long time, but a year ago he decided he wanted something more, maybe Hunter could be that.

Finally, Hunter got in the vehicle, and Wren closed the door. He strode around to the driver's side and got in.

"How did you come to live here," Wren asked starting the engine.

"Um, I met someone inside, he always talked about this town he passed through and told me about the bar. When I got out, I found my way here, and I didn't have any experience. I told Scary and Tank about my past, and I just wanted a chance. They gave me one and Bull let me move in. That was two years ago. What about you?"

"Well, I have some issues with authority, and I keep getting transferred. Powers is my last stop before I probably end up as a mall security officer. What's with you and Gregory," he asked as he darted a glance at Hunter then brought his attention back to the road.

"Gregory was married to this asshole. He was abusive, even locked Gregory in a closet and wouldn't let him out for days unless it was to work. He took exception to being denied a reconciliation because of a man like Bull. Arnold tried to kill Bull and Gregory by burning down Gregory's office, I noticed some weird shit, and I ran in."

"That was brave and stupid."

He thought about all the shit that could've gone wrong, and Hunter would've died. The thought of it bothered him more than just a human being concerned for another. Wren already liked the shy, quiet man who was more than a little socially awkward.

"That's what Gregory said too, but he's kinda adopted me since."

"I noticed."

"It's so embarrassing being around them and the Twirled Crew, they're insane."

He'd heard around town about the guys from Twirled World Ink. The rumors were rampant about the weird Crews. It wasn't anything bad, or at least he didn't see it that way.

"I don't think they're that bad."

"You almost ran, didn't you?"

He didn't see a reason to lie, and it'd be a shit way to start off dating, "I had a moment when I saw Psycho and—"

"Him and Ben have a thing about outside sex, well, sex in general. You don't see much of them."

"Sounds like all of them do."

"Crave and Twitch have been together the longest, at just about a year and a half, so maybe it's that honeymoon stage thing."

"Probably. Do you like living with all them? I've never really met people that did the whole communal living thing."

"It's great aside from the happy couples who can't keep their hands off each other. I have a room. A lock on my door. I'm never hungry or cold. It's more than I had growing up..." Hunter paused. "Besides, even being all weird, they've all become family. Communal living isn't bad, the rent and bills are super cheap. I don't even think Bull charges enough, we all don't."

"He must like having y'all there."

"That's what Gregory tells us. Bernie and Stacey, they live with Psycho and Ben, co-parenting the twins, Rage and Gunner. They're trying for another one, this time using Ben's sperm."

"That seems like an odd situation."

"Stacey and Bernie bugged Psycho for a few years to donate, but then Ben came along, the three of them decided to team up. Psycho can't say no to Ben, and Ben really wanted a few mini-Psychos running around."

"If it works for them."

He had never thought about having kids. His parents were nice enough, but not exactly the parental type, and as an only child, he hadn't spent much time around peers his own age. He'd never played with others.

They filled the rest of the trip with small talk.

He drove passed the Welcome to Powers sign and turned at the first right. There was a small business district off Main Street with a more eclectic feel. There was Vincent's Italian restaurant, along with a vegetarian/vegan place, coffee shop and used bookstore, mixed among funky little Bohemian crafty places.

"I heard Vincent's was a nice place, I haven't eaten there before."

"It's nice, it's where all the guys take their husbands on dates. I've gotten takeout a few times. Park behind Decadence Bakery, it's Ben's place, parking is shit on the street."

Wren took directions and parked in one of the two spaces. It was only a quick walk to Vincent's, Hunter walked beside him, but once they were on the street, he put distance between them.

"Are you in the closet?"

"Um, I work at Brawlers."

"Sorry, you just moved away."

"I don't want to cause trouble."

"Hunter, stop, it's fine." Wren reached out and laced his fingers with Hunter's. It wasn't like he was loud about being gay at work, but he didn't hide it either. He was sure they heard enough of the rumors.

Wren wasn't going to pretend he wasn't on a date or that he liked the odd man. He was already resigned to the fact his time in law enforcement was coming to an end. Whatever this turned out to be with Hunter wouldn't affect that. Wren flexed his arm and tugged Hunter to his side. Hunter stayed stiff beside him, yet didn't pull away so he marked it as a win.

They had a date to enjoy, he wasn't going to think about anything other than that. Tomorrow would take care of itself.

Once inside the restaurant, they were quickly seated and set up with drinks. He watched Hunter over the top of the menu. Studied the masculine angles of his face. Hunter nervously chewed on his full bottom lip, and he wanted to kiss Hunter.

A familiar gruff voice caused him to look over Hunter's shoulder to find Linus in a corner booth. Another four men were piled into the booth with Linus, and a woman was perched on Linus' thigh staring in their direction.

"Hunter," the woman called out.

Hunter turned and jumped up from the chair, and a beautiful tattooed blonde ran into his arms. She was curvy, and her tight clothes showed off each one of them.

He turned his attention to the other table to find Linus staring. A muscle in the man's jaw ticked, and he swore he saw jealousy in the man's gaze.

"Lou, what are you doing with crazies tonight?"

"Little found out I was in town and decided to kidnap me. Who's the sexy one?"

"Lou, this is Wren, Wren, this is Lou, Linus' sister."

He stood and held out his hand to Lou, but the woman didn't take it. Her eyes raked him from head to toe and then back up to his face. It wasn't a woman checking out a man, but more like a scientist would study an experiment.

"Lou doesn't do physical contact."

He nodded and dropped his arm to his side.

She turned her head and stared up at Hunter. "I thought you wanted to fuck Linus?"

He choked back an inappropriate laugh as the color drained from Hunter's face, and then it blazed.

"Lou, can we pretend—"

"No, we can't pretend we're normal. You should know that by now. Also, Mama said you haven't been to dinner in a while or on the last family camping trip."

"Please don't start, Lou, I hear enough from Linus."

"If you'd just obey and do as we say then we wouldn't have to do this."

"Lou," Linus' voice held a lethal edge, "leave him the fuck alone, let's go back to our table and leave Hunter to his date."

"He's not supposed to date someone else."

"Lou, shut the fuck up, let's go." Linus spun back toward the table. The woman stormed off in a huff. "Hunter, I'm sorry to interrupt your…date."

Wow, the disdain in Linus' tone when the man said *date* was clear.

"It's fine, I don't mind a friend of Hunter's wanted to say hi."

His cheeks ached with his forced smile. Linus was a part of Hunter's life, and he knew they were going to have to at least attempt to get along, but the man wasn't making it easy at all.

"What are you and the guys doing here?"

"Little's birthday. We were going to grab food and head out to Brawlers afterward."

"Oh—"

Hunter sounded hurt, and he didn't understand why.

"You didn't mention Little's birthday."

"Bull said you had a date tonight. Little has to head to Los Angeles tomorrow night to help out Raul."

"Um, do you think that's a good idea?"

"Hunter, it'll be fine. Now, enjoy your date, and I'll call you in a few days, okay?"

"Okay," Hunter whispered.

He observed another deceptively platonic forehead kiss and Linus walked away.

"Do you want to go say hi to your friends?"

"No, it's fine, we're on a date. I'm sorry about that."

"About what?"

"Lou…they were raised with radical honesty. They never lie."

"Everyone lies, Hunter."

"Not, the Trentons. Sometimes they do it by omission, but never an outright verbal lie."

That was interesting. He'd never met people that didn't lie. He glanced at Linus and noticed the man was working hard to avoid watching them. He became curious about Linus the more he learned of the man. Unlike the first time he'd seen Hunter and Linus together he didn't feel the jealousy, just envy at the already established relationship between the two men.

Conversation ended as the server came back to the table and they ordered. He focused on Hunter and their date. Yes, Linus was a concern. But right then, Hunter was his, and he'd enjoy his time with him. He wouldn't think about the future or if what he had with Hunter was temporary or not.

5 ALCOHOL DIDN'T SOLVE EVERY PROBLEM

Linus traced the lip of the rock glass and stared longingly at the reflection of neon in the amber liquor. Since his brother, Lucky, dragged him to Brawlers two years ago, Linus had earned a reserved stool at the bar. It wasn't the oblivion of alcohol that drew him to the run-down biker bar in the middle of nowhere. It was the sexy and clumsy bartender who just happened to be there every night he was. He was too damn old for crushes, but he couldn't resist being near Hunter.

Unfortunately, the other man never showed him one ounce of interest. That didn't mean he didn't come in just to spend a bit of time with Hunter. He wrapped his hand around the glass and lifted it to his mouth, let it hover there for a moment as he watched Hunter. He downed the double and set it down, slid it toward the rail with the tips of his fingers.

The feminine and always smiling Twitch stepped up, refilled the glass with another two fingers of bourbon.

"That's your fourth, blanket boy, wanna talk," Twitch asked, he set the bottle aside and placed his knobby, little elbows on the bar.

"I ain't here for therapy."

"Well, anyone else I wouldn't care, but you're sort of like family. So, spill."

He involuntarily glanced over Twitch's shoulder to Hunter.

"Oh, is that your problem? Got a thing for our resident baby bear."

"Don't start your bullshit, Twitch."

"You know he's dating someone, right? Dude's sexy as fuck in uniform."

"I'm gonna put you over my fucking knee."

"You're cute and all, but I don't think Crave is really into threesomes, you never know though."

"Like Crave would look at anyone else. It's disgusting."

"Just because you, Mr. Anti-Monogamy, can't fuck man or woman for more than one night doesn't mean others are nasty with their embracing of commitment."

"I didn't say I had an issue with commitment. I just find it odd and unnatural."

"What's unnatural about being in love and wanting to be with that person?"

"Are we forgetting Tank, Scary, and Elijah? They have a strong as fuck relationship."

"So, is that something you want, a ménage marriage?"

"You're not giving up on this are you," he asked, then slammed back his drink and tapped the bar for another one.

"I hate when people do that, and you know it."

Linus grinned at Twitch's cute little purr.

"Fill it, and I'll answer your question."

Twitch couldn't fill the glass fast enough. If anything, Crave's boy was nosy.

"I don't know what I want."

"You do know, you just waited too damn long now he's got a hot cop sniffing around."

"Don't remind me."

He couldn't deny Wren was one sexy fucker and Hunter was cute and sweet. Wren would be lucky to have Hunter.

He slammed back the double and raised a brow as he held out his glass. Twitch reluctantly filled it again.

"I'm not driving you home."

"Don't worry about me, Twitch, I can…"

"You even think about driving, and I'll sic Scary on you."

It was all Twitch said before he turned to take care of a couple a few stools down.

He felt the effects of the alcohol, his head began to float, and his limbs felt heavy. Without a doubt, the minute he stood up the world would tilt on its axis. There was no way he'd drive, he could call Lucky or Priest to come out and get him.

He glanced up to find Hunter watching him. Hunter's thick brows were drawn together, and the man looked concerned. He'd studied Hunter so many times he could pick out the smallest flicker of emotion. Hunter's history wasn't a mystery to him. He knew the man did time for a youthful mistake. Young kid without many options and Hunter had a valuable skill set. One he'd used a few times over the years.

If it wasn't for the fact Hunter was on probation for another few years, he'd offer the man a job, but until then they worked it out.

He scrubbed his hand over his mouth and then rested his jaw on his palm.

Twitch was right, he'd waited too long, and another man moved in on the man he'd started to consider his. He had tried to play it slow for a reason. Hunter was skittish, didn't date, and spent most of his free time hunched over his laptop. The man was sweet as could be and completely out of his league.

He was an asshole. Didn't know what not to say. If it was in his head, he said it without regret. His parents believed in radical honesty. They had only two rules growing up. One: Don't lie. Two: Don't have the cops come to the house.

Which was damn smart, no rules meant nothing really to rebel against. Except when he'd turned twenty-one he'd attended the Atlanta Police Academy. He'd never seen his mother Lily as disappointed as when she'd learned he was going to be a cop. It lasted three years before he'd butted heads with his Captain one too many times and he'd quit. He'd worked at a private security company as a bodyguard for a few years before he'd struck out on his own. Four years later he was doing well, even if his ragtag group butted heads worse than the Brawlers and Twirled Crews combined.

He sipped at his drink and decided it would be his last. He unlocked his phone and scrolled through his contacts until he reached Lucky's, he was about to tap the screen.

"If you call Lucky away from his man at one a.m., he'll kill you," Hunter warned.

"I know he won't be asleep." He was proud that his words weren't slurred. It was lucky for him he had a pretty high tolerance, but that didn't mean he wasn't drunk.

His gaze fell to Hunter's mouth. He'd never seen a man with lips that pouted quite that much before. He'd kill to find out if they were as soft as they looked. Hunter always smelled like Linus' favorite incense. He shook his head and went back to getting ready to call his brother.

"He might not be asleep, but he sure as hell is busy. Hang out and I'll take you home."

"I need my truck."

"Gregory and Bull came in Bull's truck tonight. I'll have Bull follow me to your place and then I can ride home with Bull."

"You sure?"

"Just hang out another hour until we close."

"I can do that."

"I didn't give you a choice."

"Bossy."

"I have my moments," Hunter muttered.

He watched the man slip from behind the bar and tracked Hunter until the man came up beside Bull. Bull was in his usual position at the door. Psycho was in the far corner. Psycho was tall enough to see the entire room. Scary and Tank were in a booth positioned on either side of Elijah.

All the years he'd been around the crews, and he still felt separate. Lily had taken a position of foster mother to the crew's, just as Peaches had. Still two years after he'd started hanging around full-time, he didn't exactly feel like he belonged.

Since he had a ride home…might as well enjoy it. He finished off another drink, then another until Twitch yelled last call.

His limbs were heavy, and he rested his chin in his hands to keep from face planting on the bar top. He closed his eyes and opened them to find the room spinning.

"Is the room moving or is it me," he asked. He snorted at his slurred words.

"Come on, lightweight, let's get you home."

A thick arm curved around him and as he predicted the floor seemed to go out from under him.

"Whoa, shit, Linus, put your arm around me. Thirty minutes and you can be in bed."

"You gonna join me, beautiful?" He wrapped his arms around the taller man.

"Twitch should've cut you off three doubles ago."

He snorted as they weaved out of the bar. The cool night air blew across his heated face.

"Where are your keys?"

"Front pocket."

"You going to get them for me?"

"Nope, it's the only way I'll ever get you in my pants."

Hunter laughed. "You've had way too much to drink."

Hunter reached into his pocket, and he nearly groaned as the man's hand brushed against his dick. The touch was fleeting but more than enough to get his mind headed places it shouldn't.

He bit his tongue to keep from saying anything else. He didn't need to be reminded he was nothing more than a friend. Hunter had a man. One that was probably nicer and more charming than him. He sighed as he let Hunter help him into the passenger seat of his truck. Hunter and

Bull exchanged a few words, then the door slammed, and he closed his eyes and let his head fall back.

He was tired, and it wasn't just the alcohol. He pushed a heavy breath between his lips and relaxed.

"Linus, wake up," Hunter's voice in his ear. "Come on, you're home."

Hunter's smooth cheek caressed his, and he turned his head, inhaled the musk of sweat. Part of his brain screamed for him to stop, but he didn't listen as he leaned back. Hunter's breath was warm against his mouth.

He raised his hands to push his fingers through the soft, thickness of Hunter's hair. Felt the strands teased the hollows between his fingers.

"Linus, you're—"

He didn't want excuses. One kiss, that's all he wanted. He pushed his lips to Hunter's and gently sucked at the lush curves. Fuck, he'd never felt anything as soft. Hunter gasped, and he took advantage—he slipped his tongue inside. Licked along Hunter's tongue, traced the edges of his teeth. He groaned at the taste. He fisted his hands in Hunter's hair and deepened the kiss.

For what could've been only minutes, Hunter leaned into him. The warmth of Hunter's big body seeped into his and then Hunter was gone.

"What...let's get you inside."

He opened his eyes to find Hunter avoiding his gaze. "I'm..."

"We need to get you in bed, okay?"

"Yeah, okay."

He felt the moment Hunter pulled away from him, not physically, but emotionally. Their easy friendship ruined with one kiss. Drunk or not, he should've known better. He let Hunter take him inside his house.

"I like your place."

"Thanks."

He looked around the room. It was his sanctuary. No one ever came there, and he never brought anyone home. His ceilings were upholstered with Saris that his mom had brought home from India. A colorful quilt of patterns and textures. A dim light turned the mirrored Saris into twinkling stars.

"Where's your room?"

He nodded toward the hall. The trip didn't take too long. His place was a small cottage out in the middle of nowhere. Only trees to be seen in every direction.

"It's at the end of the hall."

His bedroom door stood open. He'd dreamed of having Hunter in his room, and in his bed for a long time. That wouldn't happen now. He was lowered to his platform bed that rested in the middle of the room.

"I can take care of myself now."

"Just let me…"

"No, I'm fine. Thanks for bringing me home."

His heart was breaking, and he had never anticipated he would experience the pain of that in his life. He had kept himself separate and unemotional in his past hookups especially the ones over the last few years. Hunter was the only man he wanted, and he couldn't have him, he loved a man who wouldn't see him.

"At least let me help you take your shoes off."

Hunter knelt on the floor and lifted his jeans to unzip his tactical boots. A cascade of dark curls hid Hunter's face.

"You're so beautiful."

"Linus."

"I'm going to sleep."

He fell back onto his mattress.

"You can go now."

"Linus, please."

"It's fine. I just drank too much. Leave my keys on the table next to the door and lock up."

"You sure…"

"I'll be fine. Be careful going home."

"Goodnight."

"Yeah."

He was quickly left to his misery. He should get up and get some water, but he laid there with his eyes closed. He relived the kiss, pretended for a moment it hadn't been a mistake. He was thirty-two-years-old. Alone. And he'd ruined the one real friendship he had. He rolled over and tugged the blanket over him. He drifted to sleep picturing that he wasn't alone and Hunter had wanted him too.

6 IT WAS ONLY A DRUNKEN KISS

He lounged back in the rocking chair on Gideon's porch. He'd become friends with Gregory's cousin a year ago when he'd moved to town. Gideon played keyboard in the Executioners. A local band that did gigs at Brawlers a few times a month. Gideon was quiet and didn't get too nosy. Everyone called him Ghost because he tended to appear and disappear without anyone noticing.

Ghost ran a little organic farm and Greenhouse that he was just getting up and running.

"You've been here an hour, not that I don't enjoy your company, but you're usually at least a little more talkative than me."

Ghost arched a ginger brow. Ghost was one of those guys you'd call cuddly. His beard was full and long, he was handsome with kind green eyes.

"Linus kissed me."

"Not like we didn't see that one coming."

"What do you mean?"

"Linus is quiet and secretive as hell, but he's had a thing for you since I met him. His eyes track your every move when you're in the same space."

He felt his brows pull together, and he tried to remember if he'd noticed it, but he couldn't think of a single time he'd caught Linus watching him. He'd noticed the man, no one could miss him. Linus was a little on the short side, maybe five-foot-nine, Linus was broad and muscular. Handsome, maybe too handsome. Linus was the type of guy who could have any man or woman he wanted, and probably had.

"You're thinking too hard, don't hurt yourself."

He watched as Ghost worked on a bouquet for him to take to Nettie, Crave's mom. Ghost had worked as a party planner in New York. He couldn't imagine moving from a big city to a place like Powers. It had to have been a culture shock.

"You're so fucking funny."

"What's the issue?"

"I've been seeing someone, well, we've only had one date, but have spent time together."

"The deputy. Did you tell him Linus kissed you?"

"No, should I," he asked. He groaned and didn't know what to do or think. "Linus was drunk, he didn't know what he was doing. And he hasn't talked to me since it happened."

"Even so, but I think you're wrong. If you're thinking about getting serious with the deputy, it would probably be best to be upfront about the kiss, innocent or not."

Ghost was just out of a long-term relationship. Rumor was his ex-partner hadn't been the faithful type. He couldn't imagine being with someone for almost 20 years and staying through multiple affairs. Ghost didn't talk about it, and it wasn't in his nature to push. He preferred to be as invisible as Ghost.

"Are you sure?"

"I think it's best. Honesty at the beginning is the safest bet."

"I'm so confused."

It wasn't like he didn't have an initial attraction to Linus. The man just seemed to never look for a relationship of any kind unless it was temporary. Then there was Wren, the man wanted to date him. The kiss complicated his life, and he had enough of that.

"Okay, let me ask you something. What did you think when Linus kissed you?"

"I don't know, my brain sort of short-circuited. His beard was thick but soft. He tasted of whiskey. And he was warm and solid. He was gentle. I didn't expect that."

He'd laid in bed and relived the kiss. His brain wouldn't let it go. Over thinking everything tended to be a bad habit he couldn't break.

"Hunter, did you like it?"

He didn't want to admit it, but he did. "Yes, I didn't want to stop. He looked so hurt when I pulled away. Linus never looks sad. Grumpy and pissed off, but never sad."

"Then maybe you'd like to date—"

"But I like Wren. He's smart. Funny. He doesn't make me feel clumsy and awkward. He's gorgeous."

"Then you have a decision to make."

"What decision?"

He knew what Ghost would suggest, but he didn't know if he wanted to hear it.

"Which one do you want to have more, Wren or Linus, or," Ghost paused and set the paper-wrapped bouquet aside.

"Or what?"

"Or do you want to date them both?"

"I couldn't…there's no…"

"Scary, Elijah, and Tank make it work. Who says there's one right person? Now, I don't think I could do the whole ménage thing, but why not you?"

"Because I'm…me."

"Hunter, you're a good-looking guy. You're smarter than any one person should be. You're sweet and caring. Yeah, you're a bit clumsy and awkward, but there's nothing wrong with that."

"But I don't think Wren and Linus even like each other."

"Then do an open…"

"I don't think I could do that. What if I give too much attention to Linus and then Wren feels ignored, or vice versa? I don't know how I'd handle them seeing other people. I don't think I'm the type to get jealous, but what if I am?"

"You're over thinking, and you're going to give yourself a panic attack. I'm not saying it's something you can or should do."

"Then why the hell did you mention it, now, all I'm thinking is I like Linus. Yeah, he's a little grumpy, but he's always been nice to me. He doesn't make me feel less than. He brings me in on jobs at Trenton Security. He called me beautiful, I'm a grown ass man, I shouldn't be beautiful, yet he says it.

"Wren holds my hand in public. He survived the Brawlers Farm Gauntlet. He didn't run when I said I did time. He's fucking gorgeous."

"You've got two gorgeous men who both seem to like you. Why not tell Wren about the kiss and see how he reacts? He should know anyway. I know it might seem old fashioned on my part, but I think the person I'm dating should know if another person kissed me."

"I can do that. I just don't want Wren to get mad at Linus. Linus was drunk."

"Which is strange, Linus never gets drunk. I've seen him catching a buzz with Lily and seem perfectly fine."

"It worried me. Linus can't do stuff like that. He's got an assignment coming up. He's got to have his head in the game. I'm not going to the hospital again."

"You'll be there."

"He said the same thing."

"When Linus calls needing help you never hesitate."

"He's my friend, and I haven't had many of those until I moved here."

"Just have a talk with Wren."

"Okay. Have you met someone since you've been here?" He wanted to move the conversation away from him and how he felt about Linus and Wren. It was confusing and turning his brain into knots. What he wanted wasn't normal for him. Yes, his bosses made it work, but who said he could? He didn't know if he had it in him to even try.

"Don't start sounding like Twitch. That man is obsessed with pairing me off."

"Twitch does tend to mother people. He wasn't happy for a long time, now he wants everyone to be as happy as him."

"And I appreciate it, I really do, but..."

"But what?"

Ghost sighed. "I spent two decades with someone, assumed I'd spend the rest of my life with him. I forgave his affairs. I just don't know if I want to go through that again."

"I get that, but not every person will be like your ex."

"I understand that. When it's time, maybe I'll find someone else. Just right now I'm happy as is, okay?"

"Okay."

They fell into a comfortable silence, both lost in their own thoughts. His were probably as troubled as Ghost's. He couldn't even contemplate what it would take to date two men. Scary, Tank, and Elijah made it look easy. He knew they fought, but they enjoyed the fights. They never stayed mad at each other for long. He let his head fall onto the headrest of the rocking chair. First, he had to confess to Linus' kiss and hoped he didn't lose the chance with Wren or the friendship with Linus he'd come to love over the last few years.

7 WHAT WAS WREN SUPPOSED TO SAY?

Wren lounged on his back deck with a beer after a shit week and just wanted to relax. He'd had enough chaos to last him a lifetime. Last night topped it off with a naked man who attempted to break into his ex-wife's new house. Crying drunks weren't his favorite to deal with especially ones who refused to keep the blanket wrapped around them. He'd spent thirty minutes disinfecting the back seat of his patrol car.

He reached for his phone but thought twice about it. Hunter hadn't called him the last few days. He'd thought their date went great after the man relaxed and Hunter had stopped rethinking his every move and word. A second date was on his to-do list in the near future, but that didn't seem to be in the cards. He really liked the man, more than he had liked anyone in years.

"Hey."

He turned his head as he heard Hunter's voice.

"Hey, this is a surprise. I was just thinking about you."

"You were," Hunter asked nervously.

"Yes, you want a beer?"

Wren set his bottle aside and stood, he approached Hunter and brushed a kiss to the corner of Hunter's mouth. He frowned a bit when the man stepped back.

"No, I don't drink."

"Right, shit, I forgot. Can I get you something else?"

He retreated a few steps back.

"No, I don't…I wanted to ask you something?"

"Of course, ask anything."

He noticed Hunter was more nervous than he typically was and it made him a little leery. Maybe Hunter didn't want to date him. The last few weeks were great. They didn't get a lot of time together, but Wren made sure to set time aside each day to at least talk to Hunter. He had thought he'd made his interest clear.

"Did you still want to make a go of whatever this is?"

"If you're talking about dating and seeing where it goes, yes, why? If you're not into it then that's fine we can still be…"

"Linus kissed me."

Those three words didn't register for a few minutes, and then they did, he didn't exactly know what to say.

"I'm sorry, Ghost said it was a good idea to tell you. It was just a drunken kiss, so I'm sure it didn't mean anything. He said honesty was…"

Hunter had spoken so fast all the words ran together. He wasn't surprised by the kiss. He knew Linus had a thing for Hunter. He wasn't even the jealous type, but he had to admit he'd experienced it seeing Linus and Hunter's interaction at the diner.

Suddenly he realized Hunter was still talking, "Slow down and take a breath," he ordered.

He raised his arms and wrapped his hands around Hunter's biceps, steered Hunter toward the chair he'd vacated. He crouched down in front of Hunter and rested his arms on Hunter's knees.

"It wasn't like I didn't notice Linus had a thing for you. It was pretty obvious when I saw you two together. Why are you freaking out?"

"I liked it."

"And?"

Please don't let this be like pulling teeth to get Hunter to explain.

"Is this a guilt thing?"

"I don't know. Linus looked sad when I pulled away."

The man appeared far too miserable for a simple kiss. It wasn't as if they'd had the exclusivity talk and, to be honest, maybe it was too early to even ponder it. He had a long way to go to get Hunter to relax enough to accept a second date. He wanted more, he wouldn't lie to himself about that, but what he wanted didn't factor in when Hunter was tearing himself apart.

"Okay, let's do this, start from the beginning."

Hunter took a deep breath and then exhaled slowly. "Linus came into Brawlers like he always does. Sits on his usual stool. What wasn't normal was he drank a lot more than he usually did. I drove him home after we closed. When I went to help him out of his truck, he kissed me."

"Did you want to kiss him?"

He didn't understand why he asked, but whatever Hunter had going on in his head was most likely being blown out of proportion with insecurity and an unhealthy dose of guilt.

"I don't know…I didn't want to stop."

"Then we stay friends."

"No, I don't…"

"Tell me about Linus."

He lowered to the porch and rested his arms on his bent knees.

"He's the oldest and always felt left out. Lucky and Lou are more like Lily and Damon. Free-spirited. He didn't have the easiest time growing up. Him and the twins were sort of ostracized for being different. I think that made him try to fit in—to be as different from the rest of them as he could. I think that's why he initially joined the Atlanta PD."

"And that didn't work out for him?"

He'd admit to himself that he was curious about Linus. The man was undoubtedly exceptionally handsome. He'd had a moment of attraction when he'd seen Linus in the diner. Although, Linus didn't seem to like him very much— maybe that was because he was interested in the man Linus wanted.

"He's not much on rules. He liked going rogue a little too much, and that hasn't changed."

"Keep going."

"I always liked him, but…"

"But what?"

"He doesn't believe in monogamy."

That surprised him, Linus seemed interested in something with Hunter. A thought struck him, and he got to his knees, pushed into the space between Hunter's legs.

"What are you doing?"

He raised his hands and tucked Hunter's hair behind his ears. "Answer a question for me, don't think about it, just answer with the first thing that pops into your head, okay?"

Hunter nodded.

"Do you want Linus?"

"Yes, but…"

"No buts, Hunter. I wanted the truth and don't regret admitting it. Linus is sexy."

He closed the distance between their mouths and sucked gently at Hunter's bottom lip.

"Maybe you'd…"

"Nope, you're just as sexy." He stroked his hands down Hunter's chest, over the curve of his stomach, and lower to grip Hunter's hips. He pushed the cotton of Hunter's t-shirt up with his thumbs and ruffled the thick hair covering Hunter's abdomen.

An image formed in his head of Linus and Hunter, his cock jerked and hardened. Short and stocky Linus, and tall, hairy Hunter made a fucking sexy fantasy. As he kissed Hunter until the man started to moan, he analyzed his sudden, odd desire. He wasn't a prude, but he'd never had any interest in threesomes. One man was fine for him, but maybe it had possibilities.

He deepened the kiss and pressed Hunter back into the chair.

"Do you want Linus and me," he asked as he nipped at Hunter's lush lips. Hunter's stubble rough against his skin.

Hunter's arms twined around his neck, the man's fingers tentatively played with the hair at his nape.

He pushed Hunter's shirt all the way up and lowered his gaze to take in the thick hair covering Hunter from waist to collarbones. That was fucking sexy. He always loved hairy men. So perfect.

"You going to answer me, baby?"

"I shouldn't, but I do."

Hunter's voice barely above a whisper, hesitant. He sensed Hunter waited for him to push him away. That had never crossed his mind. He couldn't and wouldn't deny his attraction to either man. Linus remained a mystery, but he was interested in getting to know the man.

"Why shouldn't you," he asked.

"I'm me."

"There's nothing wrong with you. You're beautiful and sweet. I wanted to get to know you from the moment I spotted you. Those sexy glasses. Cute little frown."

He smiled at the blush that stained Hunter's sharp cheekbones.

"Don't get me started on these deep dimples…" He kissed one scruffy cheek then the other. "In your cheeks when you smile. It embarrasses you when I give you compliments, you gotta get used to it. I'll probably do it a lot."

"You and Linus…"

"Me and Linus, what?"

"The compliments are too much."

"Accept them, Hunter. What's so wrong with me or Linus telling you the good things about you?"

Hunter hunched down, and the man's hair shielded his face.

He placed his fingertips under Hunter's chin and urged the man to look up.

"You need to talk to Linus."

"He hasn't talked to me in a week."

"He was drunk, you probably didn't react well to the unexpected."

"He's off on an operation for a week. He won't contact me since he didn't ask me to help like he normally does. I called Gage, and he wouldn't tell me anything either."

"Is that unusual?"

"Yeah, everyone's instructed that if I ask, I'm to know where they are."

"Then why don't we plan for when he comes back, and we'll talk to him."

"Why?"

"If we're going to make this work between the three of us, shouldn't we all talk about it?"

"Why are you taking this so well?"

"I don't know, maybe it's because I like you and I won't say I don't find Linus to be an attractive man. I've never thought about a threesome, even if it was just for fun, but I can't deny I feel this could be a good thing, odd, but good.

"Want to stay for dinner? We can consider it our second date."

"Okay."

Wren smiled as he gave Hunter one more kiss and tugged at the hair on Hunter's belly. He wanted the man, but he also didn't want to rush into sex. Being with Hunter needed to be about more than that. He sensed Hunter needed more—to be loved. He could see himself falling for Hunter, but the question was could he see himself falling for Linus too. He stood, took Hunter's hands and pulled him to his feet. Soon enough they could deal with Linus. Until then, he'd learn more about Hunter, and somehow they could come up with a plan to make it work for all three of them.

8 HIS OPERATION WENT NUCLEAR

He secured his vest and looked around their temporary situation room. He didn't want to deal with the man standing across the room from him. Camden Pelter. His old Captain from his days on Atlanta PD who now worked with the Georgia State Police. The man hated him, and the feeling was mutual. His operation was going nuclear right in front of his eyes.

"Trenton."

"Don't fucking start. We've been trying to get the feds involved in the Thorpe case for years. They just keep turning their noses up."

"I know that, don't think I don't, but we've got new evidence."

"What upstanding straight, white fucker…"

"That isn't how." Camden scrubbed his hands over his face and his shaved head. "Listen, I'm not fucking arguing with you. You're from Powers, your firm is located there. You're in the best position to work with me on this."

"You mean you want me to go undercover, unofficially at that, and put my fuzzy ass on the line so you can have plausible deniability when all this shit explodes."

"Not true, I can't send in one of mine. I sure as hell don't know who I can trust. We need someone who can give us an in, and you're in a unique position."

"And what might that be?"

"Familiarity."

"Motherfucker, have you met me and I know damn well you looked my family up. Thorpe would rather spit on me and mine than look at us. Lily attempted to castrate him in high school, and he's held a grudge since."

"We may have an ally for you."

"And who is that?"

"Wren Gramble."

He snarled at the name. That sexy fucker had the man he wanted. He sure as hell didn't want to work with him.

"Not a fan."

"You hate everyone, Trenton. He's the newest deputy. He hates authority. And…"

"He's gay."

"Not what I was going to say, but, yes, something to make him more willing to be our eyes and ears."

"I won't bring someone in."

It wasn't just the fact of him not wanting to work with his competition. No, he also had experienced a fleeting surge of protectiveness at the thought of Wren's ass being put on the line. He knew what would happen if Thorpe discovered a traitor in his ranks. It wouldn't be the first time a deputy was the victim of an unsolved murder.

"Linus, we need this. Thorpe has always been unstable, but it's gotten worse. Peaches making his life hell isn't helping."

"I have no control over Peaches. Thorpe is making our Crews…"

"I don't have to be told. Scary nearly took my damn head off."

He smirked at the thought of Scary taking Camden down. It was a badly kept secret that Scary Sheridan the owner of Brawlers was related to law enforcement. One thing that wasn't done in Scary's presence was mention it. They two men hated each other, well, Scary hated Pelter and didn't trust the bastard as far as Scary could kick his ass.

"So, you're spreading the word?"

"My cousin is an asshole and when he saw me in Powers, let's just say it wasn't a happy reunion."

"Scary doesn't like anyone other than his husbands."

"True. So, you in, because if not I'm out of options."

"I'm the bottom of the barrel?"

"I had to torch through the bottom to get to you."

"Fuck, I'm feeling the love."

Him and his Crew were loose cannons, law enforcement didn't want to work with them, and that was fine with him and the guys. The less interaction they had with cops, the better they liked it. It didn't help half his guys were lucky not to have sheets a mile long.

"My office tomorrow."

"I'll think about, now, get the fuck out."

"Always good to see you, Trenton."

He watched Camden until the man exited his trailer.

"I don't trust him, boss." Livingston better known as Liv came up beside him.

He turned his head to look up at the man, the harsh scarred angles of his face made worse by the dim lights. Liv was the man to have in your corner, but those who didn't know Liv tended to run the other way when Liv showed up.

"I don't either. What's your take?"

He checked his Glock, slid it into his thigh holster, and grabbed several clips then slipped them into his vest.

"From my intel over the last year, Thorpe's about to pull some major weight. I had Little check him out, the man's pulling in six figures a year. The amount of drugs funneling through Power's fucking astounding. Bill's becoming a problem though. He's showing his ass and drawing way too much attention."

"He about to be taken out?"

"Thorpe's a bastard, but I can tell you money's everything, and Bill serves a purpose for the time being."

"What did you find out about his sons?"

"Derrick seems to be a good kid. Keeps his nose clean. Little's volunteer gig at the community center has him spending time with Derrick. As far as we can figure he doesn't have a clue what his old man his doing.

"Craig's only three. Thorpe's wife doesn't have much to do with them. Spends most of the time shopping. Another attention catcher."

"So, what do you think I should do?"

"Boss, I think we should take his ass out and make it permanent."

He nodded as his team gathered and they went over the takedown plan. Going on retrieval operations wasn't his usual job, but they were short on men. Hunter was right, he needed to bring in at least one more body. He knew a bounty hunter from his PD days, and the man helped out on occasion but nothing on a permanent basis. It might be smart to give him a call. Raul was a vicious fucker with no damn mercy, and Raul took anyone down with extreme prejudice.

"We're in and out, no heroics. Bastard is heavily armed, and his sheet tells us he ain't afraid to pull, no matter if you're wearing a badge or not. I want constant contact. Check-ins at every stage. I won't visit one of y'all families tonight, is that understood?"

"Yes, sir," his team answered scatted to take positions.

"Liv, keep an eye on Gage, I didn't want him along, but I had no choice."

"I got him, no worries."

He pushed out a heavy breath and got his head in the game. They'd planned their OP down to every contingency for the past week. He trusted his team to do their jobs. He picked up his 12 gauge, pumped it and followed his team. It was game time.

■■■

All hell broke loose, his ear piece went crazy, and he noted each voice as he went room to room. A woman screamed, a baby cried, and he ducked into the room. A girl, probably no more than eighteen, was huddled between the bed and the wall. Her face wet with tears. A small bundle held tight to her chest.

"Fuck, Liv, you copy?"

"Yes, sir."

"Southwest window, double time it, over."

"Copy, ETA five, over."

"Honey, I need you to get up, you're going out the window."

He turned and put his back to her, he raised the butt of the shotgun to his shoulder. He listened to the window slide open. The creak of wood and a pop as paint gave way signaled Liv was in charge of the woman's exit. The house was an old, one-story out in bumfuck, nowhere.

"Boss?"

"Get her out, head back to base. Team, do you copy?"

Murmurs of affirmative let him know everyone was on.

"Fall back, I got this."

He heard dissension.

"Do as I say or find another fucking job?"

They were a team for a reason, no one else wanted them.

"Boss, you got ten before I come back. Fire me, I don't give a fuck."

He glanced back to see Liv disappearing with the girl and baby. He kept his steps slow and steady, he peeked around the door frame, first right and then left. He stepped into the hallway and kept his back tight to the wall, checking his blind spots as he went.

The door in front of him exploded, shards of wood flew in every direction. He hit the floor and rolled into the nearest room. He hissed as he pulled a large sliver from his forearm.

"Motherfucker, I ain't got time for this shit, just give up."

"I don't give a fuck if you're a cop or not, you come near me, you're dead."

He snorted, a cop he wasn't.

"There's no fucking way you're getting out of here still breathing, make it easy on yourself and give up."

Another blast tore through the wall next to him and fire erupted through this left shoulder. He gritted his teeth to keep from letting the bastard know he was hit. He heard a board creak behind him on the other side of the wall and lunged forward, rolled to his back as he aimed. As he pulled the trigger pain infused his chest. The several rounds pierced his vest. He compressed the trigger, and the man flew through the air.

He coughed, and he tasted blood, he collapsed back on the floor. His back arched as pain took over everything.

"Man down, call 9-1-1, now!"

"Someone call Hunter."

"No, Wren, call Wren." He coughed as he gagged on the thick metallic taste. "Not Hunter alone."

"Fine, I'll take care of it, boss, but Hunter is a gonna kill me."

Shit time for humor on Liv's part, the man wasn't good at it. His last thought was of Hunter. The way Hunter looked when he kissed him. The regret in his beautiful eyes. He didn't get a chance to say he was sorry.

"Where the fuck are the EMTs? We need them now!"

Liv's voice faded, the pain ceased, and all went black.

9 THIS WASN'T A FRIENDLY VISIT

Shit, it was a homicide in the making, and he jumped from bed before the pounding on the door could wake Bull. It was only nine a.m. and whoever was visiting didn't know the before Noon threat. He pulled on a t-shirt as he ran from the room and threw open the door.

He froze as he found Wren and Liv on this porch. Liv looked like hell and Wren didn't look much better. Wren was also still in uniform.

"What happened?"

"Hunter, can we come in," Wren asked.

The man was being too formal.

"Where's Linus?"

"Hunter, please." Liv scrubbed his hands over his face. "Can we come in and talk to you?"

"No, you can damn well tell me now, where is he?"

"We had an OP go nuclear last night." Liv took a deep breath. "It…"

"Is he—" He couldn't finish the question. His body shook, and tears burned his eyes. "Don't bullshit me, Liv, it isn't your style."

"Our bounty was armed with armor piercing rounds. Linus' vest was shredded by several shots. We lost him at the house, we performed CPR until the paramedics arrived. They were able to get his heart going again on the way to the hospital."

"When was this?"

He locked his knees as they attempted to give out. Time enough later for him to lose his shit and curl into a ball but until then, he had to pretend to have his head on straight.

"2300 hours, last night."

"Why the fuck wasn't I called?"

Even as he asked the question he knew the answer, Linus had told them not to, and instead, Wren was notified. It was the only reason for Liv and Wren to be on the porch together.

"He told us to call Wren, he didn't want you alone when you were told."

"Stupid motherfucker! Is he awake?"

"Um, in and out, when he's conscious he wishes he was dead."

"Damage?"

"Punctured lung, nicked liver, broken ribs, the angle—"

"Does he need to know this," Wren barked the question.

"We don't lie to Hunter. The angle of penetration saved his heart…barely."

"Who went to Lily's?"

"Gage informed her earlier. I had some trouble hunting Wren down. He was on patrol."

"Then why did you—"

Liv's scarred cheek distorted what Liv tried to pull off into a small, apologetic smile filled with compassion. Some people might look at Liv and run the other direction as fast as they could, but he knew Liv was a good man—the best one to be at Linus' six.

"Hunter, we wanted to call you as soon as it happened. Linus wanted to make sure your man was with you when you were told. I regret not telling you sooner, but—"

"You didn't have a choice. I got to get dressed. You can wait in the kitchen."

When Wren went to grab his arm, he stepped back and hurried to his room. He was just pushing down his pajama bottoms when he felt someone else in the room. He turned to find Wren standing in the doorway.

"Hunter, it's going—"

"I should've been first to know. If I hadn't left him, if I had just talked to him about the kiss. This wouldn't have happened."

"Get dressed, and we'll take you to the hospital."

There was an odd coldness to Wren's tone that the man had never used with him before. "Wren…"

"I get it, you're upset and pissed off, nothing I say will make you feel better until you see him. So, get dressed."

He was left alone like he always was. He stripped off his bottoms and pulled a pair of jeans from his dresser. He dressed quickly. The minute he'd moved into Bull's house he'd had a deep sense of belonging—he'd come home. He wasn't that weird kid his parents didn't quite know what to do with or how to love him. He wasn't the terrified nineteen-year-old walking into prison and just trying to survive by any means necessary. He had father-figures, people he considered brothers and sisters, nieces and nephews.

He swiped roughly at the tears that streamed down his cheeks. Linus made him feel normal and wanted, so did Wren. He'd come too close to losing one of them. Could he take the chance on two men in dangerous careers, especially when one of them seemed to have a death wish?

Quickly he gathered his phone and bag, made sure his keys were inside and hurried to go find Wren and Liv so they could get going. He wanted to be at the hospital as soon as possible.

■■■

Hunter rubbed his tired eyes as he sat beside Linus' bed. Linus had woken up a few times in the last few hours, but he'd been in so much pain they increased his pain medicine, and Linus went right back to sleep. Wren left after Liv and him dropped him off, said he was going home to get some sleep but would be back later.

Wren hadn't tried to kiss him, just left.

"My lazy ass brother still not awake?"

"Hey, Lucky, how's Lily and Damon?"

"Dad's trying to get mom to get some sleep. He set her up in bed with her bong and some hot tea."

He smiled, it was the little things in life that made Lily happy.

"She was pissed earlier."

That was an understatement, Liv had barely kept Lily in check when the doctors tried to kick her out of the ER exam room. He knew Lily had a temper when she went into Mama Bear mode, yet he'd never quite seen her that pissed off. The woman had always carried herself with a calmness unless her mother-in-law was around and then all bets were off.

"Mom never approved of Linus and his cop thing, she's all Free Love and Pacifism. She thought if he just found a safe, hippie-friendly job—"

Hunter snorted, "That's not Linus. He loves his job."

"He also has a death wish."

He didn't like his own thoughts voiced aloud. Linus had a tendency to take risks he didn't have to, but he never put one of his crew on the line.

"He's just overworked. He needs to bring in a few more guys. His team is too small."

"Linus doesn't trust anyone, and it's taken him awhile to build a team he could deal with."

"His team is crazier than him."

"Have you eaten," Lucky asked.

"No, I just leave to grab a coffee and come back."

"I'll run down and get you something, Linus won't like if you're hungry."

"Why—"

"Don't play stupid because I for damn sure know you're not. Part of you fucking knew Linus wanted you. Always has since the minute he saw you at Brawlers."

"Why didn't he ever say anything?"

"You're kinda oblivious, Hunter."

"Get the fuck out, that was my business," Linus' voice sounded gravelly.

He surged to his feet and took Linus' face in his hands, his beard rough against his palms.

Lucky snorted "You were too fucking ball-less to say anything."

"Get out."

His mouth hovered over Linus' and didn't pay attention when Lucky left. His lips shook as he placed a soft kiss on Linus' and another.

"You're hiring more people."

"Okay. I think I need more meds."

He didn't look away from Linus' pale face as he grabbed the nurse call button and pressed it.

"I'll never be last to know again."

"Promise. Don't let them give me too much, I don't want to sleep."

"You need to sleep so I can take you home."

"What about—"

"We'll talk about that later."

"Hunter, does he need more medicine," Linus' nurse, he thought he remembered her name was Emma, asked.

"Yeah, he doesn't want as much though. Said he didn't want to sleep."

"*He* is right here."

He made note that getting shot made Linus grumpier than normal.

"Your man's cranky, is that a good sign?" the nursed asked.

"He's always cranky."

A feminine laugh made him smile, and Linus chest rumbled, then ended in a groan of pain.

"I'll go hunt down the doctor to order a lowered dose."

"I'll keep him distracted."

"Not too distracted, Hunter, we do have rules around here."

"You're funny for a nurse."

"I try. Behave until I get back."

He smiled as she left the room.

"Hunter?"

He straightened as Wren's voice sounded behind him. Shit, Wren stood in the doorway in jeans and t-shirt.

"He's awake."

"Yeah, just woke up, the nurse is going to find a doctor to lower his pain medicine."

Wren stepped inside and let the door close, he strode across the room and took the spot on the opposite side of the bed.

"You look like shit."

"Thanks, that's what getting shot four times gets you."

He'd punch Linus when the man was back on his feet. For now, he'd let the man be an asshole.

"Where was your team?"

"I told them to fall back."

Of course he did, he owed Linus two punches, but he stood back and let Wren and Linus work out whatever was going on.

"And why the hell would you do that?"

"I'd rather take the hit than one of my men."

"You're an idiot. Don't ever put me in the position of telling Hunter you almost died again."

"Better you than someone else."

"I say again, don't fucking do it again."

Then Wren hovered over Linus. Their mouths barely a breath apart before Wren kissed Linus. He waited for jealousy or anger, but nothing happened. They looked perfect together, so out of his league. Wren's strong hand grabbed his wrist and pulled him down, and Wren kissed him too.

"What the fuck—"

Linus hissed, and Hunter and Wren looked down at him. His brows were drawn together causing deep creases between them.

"Shut up, we'll talk about this later," Wren warned.

"I don't think Linus is up to a threesome after four to the torso," Lucky's said.

Hunter stood and turned to find a smirking Lucky holding trays of food.

"I saw Wren coming up, got you both something and the wounded one chocolate milk. Don't let the nurses see, they frown on patients being happy. I'll just leave these right here. Don't fuck this up, Linus, or I'll tell mom you let two son-in-laws get away."

"Fuck you."

Hunter chuckled as Lucky slipped from the room with his usual cheeky grin on his face. He was about to say something when the nurse returned with Linus' doctor. Wren motioned for him to come to him. Hunter nodded and walked around to stand beside Wren. Wren wrapped a strong arm around his waist and kissed the side of his neck.

"It'll be okay."

He hoped Wren was right. He just wanted to get Linus home. He'd worry about everything else later.

10 WHAT THE FUCK WAS GOING ON?

If one more damn nurse came into his room to poke him, he was going to call in the guys to help him escape. Two weeks passed, and it was too long to be there. Leaving his crew on their own never ended well. Last time, Little and Liv had ended up in jail, Gage had a run-in with the judge when they'd denied Little and Liv bail. And poor Pure had tried to run the office himself and ended up going after a bounty, which ended with Pure in the hospital. His freelance bounty hunter, Raul, had been pissed about Pure and beat the hell out of the jumper.

No one else wanted them, so he'd taken them in and regretted it about fifty percent of the time.

He threw his legs over the side of the bed and agony ripped through his abdomen.

"What are you doing?"

He snarled at Wren's voice. Another complication he didn't need, and he didn't know what the hell was going on with that kiss. He also didn't want to go into the whole fucked up mess Camden wanted to put them in.

"I'm leaving."

"No, you're not."

Then Wren was across the room and pushed him back into bed. He looked up into Wren's handsome face and clenched his jaw when he had the idiotic urge to kiss the man again. One he didn't freeze in shock at receiving and respond. Shit, he closed his eyes and let Wren arrange his legs on the bed.

"They said you had at least another week before we could take you home, even then you're going to need us to stay with you."

"We, us, who the hell are you talking about? I can take care of myself just fine."

"Leaving you on your own got you shot. What the fuck were thinking sending your team out?"

"I'd rather take the bullet than them."

"You're an idiot."

"Do my guys need bail?"

"Liv and Pure are at each other's throats, Gage is trying to smooth over that fucked up operation of yours, and Harm or Little, whatever you call him, and just to let you know that boy ain't little, called in some biker named Raul."

"Shit, Pure and Raul don't get along at all. I have to get to the office."

"Peaches went in to cover for you. She said you needed a lawyer on staff and would give you the price of her retainer when you got out."

"Is it that bad?"

"When I left the office, I think Peaches had Liv and Pure by the ears and giving them one helluva lecture."

He felt the involuntary twitch at the corners of his mouth. Well, he guessed someone needed to be in charge, Gage tried, but the boys didn't listen to him all the time, especially not when they were fighting. "Where's Hunter?"

"He's at your house, getting the place cleaned up and ready for when you go home."

"He should be resting."

"I told him to curl up and take a nap when he was done."

"My bed?"

"Yes, your bed."

"Why aren't you pissed about that?"

"You want Hunter, right?"

He knew what he wanted to say, but since he had met Hunter, he tried to curb his tendency to say whatever, especially when it had to do with what he wanted to do to Hunter. Telling Hunter's boyfriend he wanted Hunter wasn't on his to-do list today.

"I've heard plenty about you over the last few weeks, you don't have a filter. Just answer the question."

"Yes, but you got him first." It pained him to admit it.

"What do you think of me?"

He felt his brow furrow at the question. "What do you mean, what do I think of you?"

"Hunter loves you, you know that, right?"

"I doubt it's love."

"Quit being a cynical bastard. Our man--"

"Ours?"

"Yes, ours. You kissed him."

"Okay, I'm sorry. Okay, I'm not sorry, he was mine first."

He didn't think he liked the smile Wren gave him.

85

"Ours, you're going to have to get used to it. Hunter wants you."

Even at the announcement sadness pulled the corners of his mouth into a frown. He'd waited a long time to hear someone tell him that and it was too late.

"And you want him, I want him, and that leaves us with one choice."

"And what would that be?"

"He dates us both."

"Are you fucking insane?"

"Absolutely not, but it wouldn't just be us dating him, it would be the three of us dating…"

"You want to date me? Now, I know you're crazy."

"You've got the personality of a pit viper, but I don't think you're as bad as you let on."

"Fuc—"

Wren's mouth on his cut him off. He raised his hands and combed his fingers through the short, silky strands of Wren's dark hair. He moaned as he opened, stroked his tongue over Wren's lips. Unlike before, Linus took control. Deepened the kiss until he heard their rough breathing, Wren's sweet little moans, and he used his hands to tug Wren's head back. He took in the man's flushed cheeks and eyes at half-mast.

He ignored the pain in his ribs and chest.

"What the fuck are you doing?"

He groaned and eased backward onto the bed when his mother's voice broke into the moment. Fucking great, he released Wren's hair, and Wren laid his forehead on his chest.

"I know I raised you with no shame, but you're cheating on Hunter. I should kick your ass for this."

"Mom, I'm not—"

"Hello, ma'am, I'm Wren."

He watched as Wren stood and turned to Lily. The disgust on his mother's face was only rivaled by the sheer disdain the woman had for her mother-in-law.

"Who said I wanted to know who you were?"

"I'm dating your son."

"No, you're not, because I already picked my future son-in-law and you're sure as fuck not him."

His lips twitched as his five-foot-nothing mother slammed her fists down on her hips. She'd quickly adopted Hunter the moment Linus brought him for dinner the first time. The attention his mother bestowed on Hunter had completely overwhelmed the man, but over the last year or so, Hunter seemed to soak it up. He had a feeling Hunter was starved for love and affection. It wasn't exactly his strong suit, but he tried to touch Hunter whenever he could; give Hunter compliments.

"Linus, he's a cop. We don't fuck with or for that matter fuck law enforcement."

Linus studied the shock on Wren's face. Oh, yeah, Wren had no idea what he was in for.

"Ma'am—"

"My name is Lily, not ma'am. Now, Linus, how could you do this to Hunter, I've known that boy's wanted you since I met him."

"Mom, go catch one and relax."

"Narc!"

"Lily, I don't have the patience today."

"You never have the patience. You lock yourself away in that house of yours when you're not trying to get yourself killed. We've talked about your death wish, and contrary to popular opinion I kinda like you."

"Am I your least fucked up child?"

"No, Lucky still has that distinction for the mere fact he gave me a son-in-law and a grandson."

"We've discussed this."

"Come on, I can bribe Lou into more womb space. Find yourself a nice man, or what about the blind date I set you up on?"

"She was older than you."

"I'm not that old, Linus, I will have you know your father finds me just as flexible today as the night we met."

"Can we not go full out parental copulation tales with a newbie around?"

"You're such a prude, I raised you better than that."

"Yes, yes, I am the great Trenton disappointment."

"No, that would be Lou, but I did hear Lou maybe dating a very lovely dominatrix, I could have a daughter-in-law."

The woman's almost teenaged girly squeal brought a grin to his face. He loved the crazy woman, and he might complain about his childhood, but no one could've asked for a better mother.

"Professional or Personal?"

"I think a mixture of both, your sister does like the occasional scene or two."

"Again, not the place or time." Linus nodded toward Wren.

"If he's too sensitive about human sexuality then I definitely don't want him for a son-in-law. Now, where's my Hunter?"

"Linus' house. He was cleaning up and then going to take a nap. I was going to pick him up later and bring him back to see Linus."

"Are you going to tell him about the kiss? I won't have my Hunter lied to by anyone, not even my former parasite."

"He's well aware of the kiss, this isn't the first one."

He noticed the wheels turning in her head, and then her eyes lit up with maniacal glee. There was the light bulb moment.

"Two," she squealed loud enough to break glass. "Dear fake baby Jesus, you're now my favorite."

He braced himself as she bounded across the room and lucky for him she slowed beside the bed, then gave him a tight squeeze and a loud kiss on his forehead.

Lily spun and stared up at Wren and asked, "You're not a church goer, right, not in the closet, or, fuck, worse, a Republican?"

"No, not particularly religious, out but keep my stuff quiet at work, and definitely not a Republican."

"Oh, thank you, Zombie Jesus. Any chance you'll quit your job? It would make you almost perfect."

"No plans to quit my job."

"He's not allowed in my house, Linus."

"I'll warn beforehand."

He didn't know why he wasn't protesting the whole dating thing. He couldn't deny he had fallen in love with Hunter over the years or that he was attracted to Wren. His only concern was Hunter getting hurt if it turned bad.

"You do that. Now, he can go get my Hunter. He shouldn't be alone after Linus didn't have him informed until last."

"Mom, don't start."

"I'll go check on him. If he's still asleep, I'll call."

"Okay." Linus didn't know what else to say, but Wren kissed him one more time before leaving.

"You're going to explain this, and now."

He groaned and wished the woman would leave. He didn't have time for this or the energy.

"Break me out?"

"No, your doctor said another week, my adopted sons can handle themselves for that long."

He hoped so, but with past experience, it was going to be a clusterfuck.

11 SEEING A GROWN MAN POUT WAS SAD

Wren opened the door to Linus' house and walked inside just as the sun was coming up. His shift had been shit, and he was tired of Thorpe and all his minions. They were increasingly making his work life Hell, but right then that didn't matter. He removed his belt and laid it gently on the table beside the door and then quietly crept through the house. The light was on in Linus' office. He pushed the door open with his fingertips and found the man behind the desk. His face etched with pain. Even the paleness of his face didn't take away from how handsome he was.

Linus' beard and hair were shaggier than the first time he'd seen Linus. It still felt odd the three of them together, well, not in the way they probably wanted to be, but they had a lot to work out. First, was getting Linus well.

Hunter and him had bitched at Linus about working too many times. He knew the only reason Linus was in his office would be Hunter was asleep in the guest room.

They'd talked over the week. Nothing serious and they hadn't gotten down to what a relationship between them would be. He had a feeling Linus had avoided the conversations. The man had something on his mind, but Linus wasn't sharing, and that wouldn't work for him.

"Hunter would kick your ass if he found you in here."

"I had reports to file, cops to deal with."

"Ruled a clean shoot," Wren asked. He stepped deeper into the room with the blackout curtains. He loved that Linus kept the house dark for him and Hunter, but he also knew Linus wasn't getting as much rest as he should.

"Finally."

"Now, do you want to tell me what you're keeping to yourself?"

"Do you know a Camden Pelter?"

The question took him by surprise. He knew the name. Pelter was a stickler for law and order, but he wasn't saying appearances couldn't be deceiving. Although, if the rumor was true, any law enforcement officer who didn't follow the rules in Georgia found themselves in Pelter's sights.

"Used to be a Captain, transferred to a position at the State Police about four years ago. Mainly handles corruption cases, why?"

"Sit." Linus motioned to the chair in front of his desk. "We've got to talk."

He took a seat and raised his left leg to rest his ankle on his knee.

"Okay, spill it."

"Pelter came to see me before the OP went bad. You remember the fire at Gregory's office?"

"Unhinged ex decided to kill Bull and Gregory, the investigation was pretty straightforward. I wasn't involved, though."

"Hunter went in, he noticed someone creeping outside Gregory's building, he called 9-1-1. No one responded until the building was almost to the ground. So, me and my guys started looking into shit. The Powers Sheriff Department is a cesspool."

"I'm not going to disagree."

"Listen, Thorpe is running major weight through Powers. Either he's one of the heads of the trafficking or he turns a blind eye and takes a hefty kickback."

"You're saying, Thorpe's a drug runner?"

He almost found it laughable. The man wasn't smart enough for an operation like that.

"Drugs, humans, like I said, he's running or at least aware. His wife is going through money like crazy, she spends about what should be a Sheriff's yearly salary in a month."

Linus tossed a file onto the desk. He picked up the folder and started to thumb through the contents.

"Thorpe has a hard-on for the Twirled and Brawlers Crews, EMTs and Law Enforcement are always five minutes slower than they need to be. The calls are recorded, but dispatch waits. Crave spent a night in jail, and he came out beat to hell and wouldn't talk about it. Psycho and a friend of ours, Joker, were held without hearing. It took two days to get them medical attention.

"Rumor is Thorpe's nephew, and his friends regularly takes out their drunken temper on Harper. She's been admitted to the ER multiple times without so much as a report taken."

"I'll admit he's a bigoted fucker, and I won't deny this file makes him look dirty, but with nothing besides speculation he's golden."

"Pelter came to me wanting my help. Wanted my team to start taking a deeper look. He's aware we've been doing a bit of digging for a while now."

"It better be in an official capacity."

"Pelter doesn't know who to trust."

"So, he could hang your ass out to dry?"

He didn't like that at all. There were too many ways it could go wrong. And if Pelter wasn't what he said he was, then Linus and his team would be on the hook for some major time—if they even survived.

"Probably, but Pelter is so clean that fucker squeaks. He's got this major thing for law and order. Ain't no way he's dirty."

"I can agree with that, but what does that have to do with this?" He held up the file.

"He wants an inside man he can trust."

"There it is, wants to get me jacked up as well."

"Little would hook you up with wires and a couple of bugs for the station. Pure can blend in anywhere, so he'd shadow you during the day. That sweet face gets him out of trouble all the time. I can't send Liv in, he's had too many run-ins with Thorpe."

"I work nights, Linus."

"We're already tracking your phone and vehicle GPS."

"You're tracking me?"

He should be pissed, but he was more amused than anything.

"Yes."

"And you didn't ask me?"

"No."

Linus was a clueless man, but his man needed to be in bed. He stood, laid the folder on the desk and walked around it.

"You're going back to bed."

"I don't—"

"Hunter is always cold, let's go keep him warm, and I really need sleep."

He helped Linus stand, but as he led him toward the door, he tensed as Linus tipped sideways and landed on the edge of the desk. Linus' hands were tight on his hips as Linus pulled him between his thighs. Strong, steady hands picked apart the buttons on his uniform shirt.

"What are you doing," he asked.

"Taking your shirt off."

"I can see that."

Linus tugged the shirt from his waistband and undid the last two buttons. Linus' calloused hands slipped beneath the fabric at his waist and stroked upward. He groaned at the feel of those rough pads against his skin. His cock hardened as the contrast of soft lips and coarse beard teased one nipple, then sucked lightly. He lifted his hands to sink his fingers into Linus' hair. Where his skin was smooth, Linus was hairy.

Fuck, he did love hairy men, and he now had two all his own.

He dropped his arms to his sides as Linus pushed the shirt off his shoulders. He took Linus' cheeks in his hands and tipped the man's head back to look at him. He lowered his mouth to Linus' and hovered there as he stared into Linus' oddly colored eyes.

"You've been avoiding this all week."

"Fuck," Linus groaned. "Really, we're gonna talk about this shit?"

"Yes, listen, hurting Hunter would kill me."

"I don't plan on it. I did say I had him first."

"We going to have the who got him first conversation again?"

"It's not a conversation, it's a fact."

He couldn't resist rolling his eyes. He'd learned a lot about Linus by observation the past four weeks. Linus didn't argue. Linus didn't lie. Linus had a temper that would make a rabid bear seem tame in comparison. Linus was sweet when he dealt with Hunter. He wondered how Hunter hadn't seen Linus' interest before.

"You don't lie, do you?"

"Damage from childhood."

"Really," he asked.

"Lily's parents were involved in an open relationship. She lived in a house where they were honest about everything, but that was the one thing they kept from her. She confronted them when she thought they were having affairs."

"That would warp someone's thinking."

"Lily decided she'd never lie about anything for any reason. She raised us with this radical honesty philosophy. We told our parents everything. Conditioned from birth to say whatever was on your mind whenever, wherever it seems normal."

"But not for everyone."

"No, we were those weird hippie kids."

"I bet you were cute."

"I was."

"Oh, there's ego in there."

"No, just fact. Lucky, Lou, and me fought all the time, but we were the only friends we had. You remember in school when they asked you what you were going to do for the summer?"

"Yeah."

"Well, I dreaded that day, because I'd stand up and tell them summers at a commune. Spending a summer on the edge of the Brazilian Rain Forest so your mom can work on her thesis. Backpacking across Europe."

"I bet they were all jealous."

"Maybe, but all I focused on were the stares. It was always the three of us against the world."

"I'm an only child. My dad went to work almost every day of the week. I barely saw him. My mother had her clubs and social events. I wasn't ignored. It wasn't a bad childhood just lonely."

"I don't get that, mom was always home. Dad took us to school every day. Mom and Dad were equal in everything, from changing diapers to cooking dinner. Every night at dinner we sat around the table and discussed everything."

"Sounds nice."

"We'll see what you think when you get to go to family dinner this Sunday. Lily's patience is growing thin."

"I was surprised I hadn't seen her since the hospital."

"I told her to stay away."

"Why?"

"Why not? I talk to her every day, and she's happy with that."

"Every day?"

"Yeah."

He couldn't imagine talking to his parents every day. It was lucky if he called them once or twice a month. He was interested in seeing Linus interact with his family.

From what he'd heard about them, he was anxious to witness the Trenton craziness.

"Ready for bed?"

"I'm off for a few days, but this past week has been shit."

"They giving you problems?"

"I don't hide the fact I'm gay at work, but I don't advertise either. It's a small town, and I'm sure my past came here with me."

"You want me to send Liv and Little in?"

"No, you do know Little needs constant supervision, right?"

He'd spent only a few hours in total with Harmon Little, and the man was a menace. He was over six and a half feet of overgrown kid. He swore if you saw the man running and giggling it was best to follow him to safety.

"He's good. He's mellowed."

"He set off a glitter bomb in Liv's office."

"Shit, I didn't hear about that one. Maybe I should—"

Wasn't happening, so he cut off Linus, "Let's go to bed."

"I have to go back to the office some time."

He wasn't going to argue with a man who didn't argue, it would end in an exercise in futility. He stepped back and took Linus' hands, gently tugged him toward the door.

"Is this supposed to be the end of the conversation?"

"Yes. You won't always win because I'm always right."

"Whatever you say."

He led him to the guest room where Hunter slept, his room was across the hall, and Linus' room was at the end. He didn't know why, but he wanted his men near him tonight. Increasingly over the last few weeks, he'd realized how much he wanted this to work between the three of them.

He smiled as he found Hunter in the middle of the bed under a thick pile of covers. He'd caught Linus a few times layering them on after Hunter went to sleep. Linus and him parted, headed to opposite sides of the bed. They quickly stripped down to their underwear and slipped into bed on either side of Hunter. He scooted up behind Hunter and kissed the back of his neck. Linus' arm laid over them. Something inside him fell into place as if this was everything he'd waited for the last few years. He'd make it work. All of them deserved it, especially Hunter.

Closing his eyes, he pushed in even closer and let himself relax as he heard the birds singing outside.

12 DID HUNTER LEAVE HIS ELECTRIC BLANKET ON?

Hunter was warm, and the weight of all his blankets was comforting. He smiled to himself as he thought about all the times Linus piled the blankets on him to make sure he was always comfortable. But it was definitely warmer than usual. Did he leave the electric blanket on? His brain slowly woke up, and he started to notice things. There was a bulky and hairy body pressed to his front and a smoother, muscular one behind him. He slowly opened his eyes, and his cheek was laid on Linus' chest.

He held his breath and then exhaled. He'd gone to bed alone. Linus in his room and Wren at work. He didn't remember them coming in or curling up around him. He tensed as Wren shifted behind him and Wren's hand spread over his chest. Oh fuck, he remembered he was naked. He hadn't changed his habit of sleeping nude just because he was at Linus' place. Every hairy, not toned inch of him was locked between perfect Linus and Wren.

He needed to escape, but he had a hundred pounds of blankets holding him down, not to mention four hundred pounds of combined male on either side. His heart began to kick up an agitated beat. He held his breath again as he attempted to ease to a sitting position.

"Where you going?" Linus' voice was gruffer and sexier than normal.

He glanced up to find Linus watching him.

"I was trying to get up."

"Why?"

"I don't know."

When Linus rolled toward him, he nervously nibbled on his lower lip and watched Linus from under his lashes.

"You have to be careful."

"I'm fine, Hunter. The doc yesterday said I was healing right. If something caused me pain don't do it. Baby, I'm fine, I promise."

Linus laid his hand on his cheek, and he leaned into it. He'd watched every move Linus made over the last few weeks. He had even kept him away from the office. He didn't want Linus to go back. He couldn't do that again.

"What're you thinking?"

"I don't want you to go back."

Linus leaned in and brushed a gentle kiss across his lips, then Linus laid his forehead against his.

"I've been doing this a long time, Hunter."

"You have a death wish, Linus."

"No, I don't. But now that I have you two, I promise to be more careful."

"Promise, promise?"

"Hunter?"

"I know, I know, you're mentally incapable of telling a lie."

"Exactly, now tell me why you were really trying to get away."

He lowered his gaze to the wide expanse of Linus' bare, hairy chest.

"I'm naked."

A slow smile spread Linus' full, firm lips. He remembered how good Linus' mouth felt on his. A calloused hand stroked down his back over his ass, and he tensed. He couldn't deny he was fuzzy everywhere.

"I could tell and why's that a problem? Are you uncomfortable being naked with us?"

Us, Linus and Wren used that word a lot. They made it seemed so natural. He wanted to prove he wasn't a fuck up but knew he'd show his true colors sooner or later.

"Men have made comments about how—"

Words froze on the tip of his tongue as Linus' fingers squeezed his cheek, sinking into his crease. He arched his hips backward and instantly realized Wren's morning wood joined Linus' fingers. His dick hardened where it pressed to Linus' thigh. He moaned as Wren tugged at the hair on his chest and rolled his hips.

Linus moved his hand stroking him and Wren in tandem. Wren trembled and stretched, then Wren nipped at his shoulder. His chest felt tight like he was about to have a panic attack. Sweat beaded on his skin and Linus' fingertips tipped his head up. Linus' mouth came down on his. The kiss was slow and gentle, much like the first one Linus gave him. As if Linus wanted nothing more than to simply kiss him.

"That's sexy," Wren's breath fanned his ear.

Linus' hand disappeared, and he felt Wren jerking behind him. Linus' arm flexed, and Wren moved even closer to his back. Wren's hand wrapped around his cock, and he moaned into Linus' mouth. Linus pushed his tongue passed his lips.

He hadn't been touched in so long. He was rolled onto his back, and the covers disappeared, Linus' mouth left his and Wren's replaced it. Strong hands nudged his thighs apart. He jerked his hips up as Linus nipped and sucked at his balls. His breath shuddered as he gripped Wren's bicep with his left hand and he whimpered as wet heat surrounded his cock.

"Easy, baby, shh," Wren's voice soothed.

He opened his eyes, and he followed Wren's gaze to where Linus laid between his thighs. Linus bobbed along his length and then took it all until Linus' nose buried in his thick nest of pubes. He returned his attention to Wren.

Even with the pleasure coursing through him causing his body to arch and tighten uncertainty dampened it. He waited for the moment of jealousy—something—but it wasn't there. Wren's smooth, tanned skin was flushed and shone with sweat, and Wren's breathing was harsh. Wren stroked every inch of his, tugged at the hair on his chest and stomach, plucked at his nipples. He shuddered and opened his thighs wider as Linus massaged his hole and pushed at the muscle.

He whimpered as Wren's mouth slammed down onto his and Wren's tongue thrust deep. He focused on the rough kiss and the pressure around his cock. The end was coming too quickly. He fucked Linus' mouth as Wren bit and sucked at his lips.

He grunted as his hips lifted and fell. Wetness painted his hip, and he jerked away from Wren, looked down to find Wren's boxer briefs at the top of his thighs. Wren rutted against him. He reached across his body and gripped Wren's hip.

"Up." He licked his lips.

Wren moved quickly to sit up and knelt at the head of the bed. The man's thick cock bobbed in front of him. He flicked his tongue out to taste the pearly drops and moaned as the taste of Wren filled his mouth. He stroked his palm over Wren's hip and around to squeeze one muscular cheek. Wren's fingers fisted in his hair, and he barely had a second to prepare before Wren thrust between his parted lips. He gagged a bit as the spongy head pushed to the back of his throat. Wren took his mouth in quick, shallow thrusts.

His body jolted as Linus' heavy body rested on top of his, their cocks notched together. Linus' mouth sucked at his throat, his earlobe, and then Linus began to move. It was a fierce but easy rhythm.

"So sexy, sucking his cock," Linus gruffly whispered in his ear. "Want to fuck you while you do it."

He nodded, he would've begged if Wren wasn't fucking his mouth. It could've been seconds or minutes, Linus shifted to the side then slick fingers pushed at his hole. Linus slowly stretched him, the pressure and burn so right, it increased until four thick fingers fucked him in a brutal pace.

Linus' free hand joined Wren's, his head pushed forward until Wren's curls tickled his nose. He swallowed and listened to Wren and Linus groan in unison.

Linus weight disappeared, and he glanced out of the corner of his eye to watch Linus slip on a condom, then slick himself with more lube. Linus pushed his left leg toward his chest. Tears slipped from the corners of his eyes as Linus pushed and popped inside. It was a slow, gentle glide until finally, Linus' hips were flush to his ass.

That's when pleasure and pain converged. Wren and Linus leaned toward each other. Their mouths meshed perfectly, and he stared at them. He wrapped his hand around his cock and started to stroke. Linus and Wren matched the speed of his strokes on his cock. Linus' hand fisted in Wren's hair and wrench the man's head back, then Linus sucked at Wren's Adam's apple.

They were so perfect and sexy together, his heart pounded against his ribs, and he rolled his hips. He wanted his men to come, to see them lose themselves, and feel the heat of Linus' release inside him, taste Wren's on his tongue. Their groans and grunts joined into a cacophony of sexual bliss. Two pairs of heavy-lidded eyes fell to watch him.

He felt wanted and loved, and he hadn't realized until that moment how much he needed it. Wren pulsed against his tongue, the tang of pre-come filled his mouth and then Wren jerked.

"Shit, both my men are fucking tight," Linus growled. "You want this cock next don't you?"

Wren gave a jerky nod. Wren's cock slipped from his mouth, and he moaned at the loss.

"Fuck him, while I take your pretty ass."

"Wren," he whispered as Wren leaned down, kissing him.

Wren played with his hair, then Wren was gone. Linus slid a condom down the thickness of Wren's cock.

Wren took Linus' place between his thighs, quickly Wren pushed inside and laid on top of him, pushed him into the mattress with his weight. Wren's mouth hovered over his as he watched the emotions and ecstasy play across Wren's handsome features.

"You okay," he asked.

"So fucking good, so tight." Wren flexed his hips thrusting deeper.

He glanced over Wren's shoulder to find Linus staring at Wren's ass. From Linus' movements, he knew Linus was getting Wren ready. The sound of another condom opening preceded the tensing of Wren's body as Linus blanketed Wren's back.

"Hunter, wrap your legs around us. Fuck, all mine, both of you."

The first thrust took him by surprise. The force and power of it took his breath, then a symphony of grunts joined in perfect harmony as Linus rode them. His thrusts forced Wren deeper, when Wren followed the retreat, the glide over his prostate made him roll his eyes, and they closed.

The dance began, and Hunter was lost in the pleasure. The deep ridges of Wren's abs rubbed his cock until his balls ached. He shouted as heat spread between their bellies, and it didn't end. The push and pull intensified, and he cried out repeatedly as he forced his eyes open just in time to see Linus and Wren throw their heads back. Shouts morphed into deep, long groans. Linus and Wren powered forward once more, and their bodies were sealed together as muscles tensed. Harsh breathing mingled as they separated but only long enough for Linus and Wren to lay on either side of him.

A three-way kiss that should've been awkward felt perfect and right. That might not have been how he'd pictured finding the one for him, but he wouldn't fuck it up. They were his, and he was theirs. Linus and Wren pulled away and rested their heads on his chest. He raised his hands and teased the damp, softness of their hair. No

words were exchanged and none needed to be, it was just—
right.

13 WREN WANTED TO GO HOME TO HIS MEN

Wren's legs bounced as he checked the time for the thirtieth time in probably as many minutes. The department was quiet. They'd called him in for a second shift on his first night off when he'd wanted to stay in bed with his men. He smiled to himself at the thought. His men. Linus had been a little worse for wear. Linus had overdone it, so Hunter ordered Linus to stay in bed.

When he'd left, Hunter was taking Linus dinner in bed. He'd kissed Hunter and promised to be home soon. It had been days since he'd even gone to his apartment. He and Linus were about the same size so he'd just raided the man's dresser for sweats and t-shirts. Dropped off and picked his uniforms up from the dry cleaner.

He shifted in the chair, his ass a bit sore. Years passed since he'd bottomed for anyone, but the minute he'd felt Linus' fingers in his crease, he'd wanted it. It felt natural. The three of them together just felt right. He loved being in Linus' house—loved the routine they'd fell into. He knew they were going to have to go back to their own places soon, so, he was going to enjoy it while he could.

The darkest part of their time together was Thorpe and his bullshit. Little showed up right as he was leaving the house to drop off a wire and the bugs for the station. He'd planted them while everyone was out for dinner. It wasn't like he cared about the men he worked with, a few of them were okay, and he tolerated them.

If the Intel Linus shared was true then Thorpe needed to be taken down. It wasn't like he hadn't become suspicious over the time he'd worked for the Powers Sheriff Department. Things never quite added up. Conversations that would end when he walked into a room or went to the locker room to grab his bag at the end of his shift. Six months after he'd started, he'd made an anonymous report about Deputies who spent money a little too freely. He was comfortable, paid his bills with some left over, but this definitely wasn't a line of work someone went into for the money.

A door opening drew his attention, and he glanced over his shoulder to find one of the older deputies entering. Cabot was a first-class bastard. The man didn't attempt to censor his off-color jokes—the first to use excessive force.

"Still here," Cabot asked. "Shouldn't you be with your…" Cabot snarled.

He knew it was no secret that he was dating Hunter or the fact he'd been staying out at Linus' place. He didn't care what they thought. What he did outside of work was no one's business but his. Who he decided to date or have in his bed didn't matter.

"Waiting for my replacement."

"Well, I'm here."

"Then I'll be headed home."

"Heard you were staying out at the Trenton place."

"So?"

"You should watch the people you associate with, especially ones like Trenton. Man ain't right and I ain't just talking about who he fucks."

"Who he decides to date isn't anyone's business but his."

"Whatever."

Wren rolled his eyes as he gathered up his things. He didn't put his backpack in the locker room like normal but kept it at his desk. He stood and slung it over his shoulder.

He made his way toward the door and swore the man said *Fag* as he passed, but he kept his mouth closed even though he clenched his teeth. He pushed open the door and stepped outside.

It wasn't the first time someone had said it and probably wouldn't be the last. He really needed to find a new job, yet finding a new job meant leaving Hunter and Linus. That wasn't something he was ready to do, if ever.

What happened earlier that afternoon wasn't something he'd planned. He'd been willing to wait until they'd discussed their relationship. Expectations. Would it always be the three of them or separate? IT was out of his scope of experience. All his past relationships were one-on-one, casual or committed. Two partners never crossed his mind.

He walked down the sidewalk to his *Jeep*.

"Wren," a husky, feminine voice called out.

Lily made her way down the sidewalk. Her long, flowing skirt gave her the appearance of floating.

"Lily, what are you doing out and about this late?"

"I'm a grown ass woman, I come and go as I please."

"Never said you didn't."

"Damon is doing a lecture at some college on the west coast this week. We've spent almost every day together for thirty-five years. The house is all weird without him."

"I can see that. Did you want a ride home?"

"That would be great. How's Linus?"

"Didn't you talk to him earlier?"

"Yes, but he lies."

He chuckled as he opened the passenger door for her. He helped her into the seat and then jogged around to the driver's side. He tossed his bag in the back and jumped up into the seat.

"You know damn well Linus doesn't lie."

"It's by omission which is the same fucking thing."

"By the way, he's fine. Hunter and him were getting ready to have dinner when I left earlier."

"I normally don't give a fuck about someone's comfort, but you're new, so I'm going to be delicate about asking, are you fucking my son?"

If that's what she considered delicate, he was going to hate to know what she considered, well, not delicate. He pulled out of the spot and turned to head toward Lily's house.

"Lily, I don't think that's appropriate—"

"Fuck appropriate. My kids tell me everything, even Linus. I fostered a strong sense of openness in our family, and you should get used to it now. I only ask for the fact that Damon and I tried the whole ménage thing for several years. Neither of us is particularly jealous. I can't say the same for Linus. My son is more...traditional."

"I really don't want to know this."

There were some things you didn't need to know about one of your boyfriend's mothers, and her sexual history was one of them.

"Do you like my son?"

He quickly glanced at her then back to the road. "Yes, I like him very much."

"Good. Linus needs someone to like him, maybe love him one day. He was the normal one in our little family unit. Yes, he's not one for monogamy, but he's also not–"

"Are you saying he's a—"

"No, not a cheater. Having one partner seems unnatural. I think having multiple partners is right for him. You and Hunter seem perfect for Linus. Can I be serious with you for a minute?"

That question made him nervous, but he answered yes anyway.

"I don't think Linus has a death wish as everyone accuses, but he has nobody just his to make him cautious when he goes on operations. You and Hunter will give him something to stay alive for, thank you for that. During our conversations, I can already tell the difference, he seemed happier over the last few weeks."

"You don't have to thank me for that, Lily. I've learned a lot about Linus since he got hurt. He's intelligent, sweet with Hunter, I even like his complete honesty. I enjoy the fact that he doesn't argue."

"Usually arguments are a reason for makeup sex."

"Yes, but I've fought with almost all of the men I've dated, granted not many but most of our fights were over lies or half-truths. I don't have to deal with that with Linus."

"No, you don't. Are the three of you coming to dinner Sunday?"

"I think Linus mentioned that I'd meet everyone at dinner."

"We get together every Sunday."

"Then I guess I'll see you then," he said, he pulled up to the curb in front of Lily's house.

Wind chimes filled the night. He swore he could smell incense on the breeze. The house was quirky and stood out, but he sensed it was a happy home. Just then both their phones started beeping. He checked the message from Linus and without another word they took off toward Linus' house.

Thorpe had fucked up, he'd threatened the wrong man—Elijah.

14 NO ONE FUCKED WITH A CREW HUSBAND

Linus' house was filled with Brawlers and Twirled Crews, plus a few of the Executioners. He turned as the door opened to find Lily entering with Wren behind her. He didn't even hesitate to kiss Wren when he passed him on the way to the kitchen. Hunter was leaning against the door frame.

"I'm not gonna be fucking civil, Thorpe stepped over the fucking line. I can deal with those fuckers posted outside my bar, but you don't threaten my husband," Scary roared from his spot behind Elijah.

Elijah was cradled on the huge man's lap.

Thorpe and whoever was with him had asked questions about both the Twirled and Brawler Crews, even brought up a few of the Executioners. All of them, including him, had spent at least a few nights in one of Thorpe's holding cells. He was sensing a frame job, so that's why he'd called in Peaches. The woman had friends in low places and willing to use them when necessary. Thorpe had fucked up enough when he'd cornered Elijah, but he'd brought up the kids, Princess, Juvie, and Matty. Visits from Social Services would be a distraction tactic, while Thorpe figured out how to take the Crews down.

"I'm not saying shit, Scary, but, fuck, I got an operation in the works. Everyone riding in to take out Thorpe is gonna bring the fucking heat down on us," Linus said.

Brody, Elijah's brother, leaned back against Trouble's chest. Thankfully, the Twirled Crew wasn't as volatile as the Brawlers, he couldn't say the same about the Executioners. He could practically see Joker ready to tear someone's head off. Joker wore a permanent frown. Unless the man was brawling, he'd never seen the man smile. Now, his exact opposite, Ghost, sat calmly on the floor playing with Princess, Brody's daughter.

Ghost was Gregory's cousin, Gregory was married to Bull, both of which were sitting close by Ghost and Princess, but were thankfully quiet.

Fuck, there were too many people in his house. All he'd wanted to do was spend the evening with Hunter and Wren.

Wren getting called into work had cut their day together short.

"So, what the hell happened," Lily spoke up as she took a seat on the coffee table and crossed her legs.

"At about six p.m., Elijah was pulled over on his way back from Atlanta by Thorpe, and I believe from Elijah's description, Cabot. He was detained on the side of the road for two hours as he was interrogated. His phone was confiscated, and he was placed in the back of Thorpe's cruiser. He was asked repeatedly—"

"My husband was interrogated, he was—"

"Scary." He sent Tank a pleading look, and the man wrapped his arm around Scary.

"What I'm about to share has to stay between us, understood," he asked as he looked around and met everyone's gaze. When everyone nodded, he took a deep breath.

"Before I got hurt, I got a visit from my old Captain. He's moved to the State Police. Pelter sent me some info, they have evidence Thorpe's involved with trafficking."

"Drugs or people," Joker asked.

"Both, the operation is need to know. Pelter doesn't know who he can trust. He's working with a small task force of FBI and DEA agents. I don't know names, and I didn't ask. Suffice it to say, there's enough evidence to warrant a very close look. Me and my team are working in an unofficial capacity." He nodded to Liv.

The big man stepped up to his side. "We've been looking into this for a while. Shit doesn't add up and with Lucky's accident, the fire at Gregory's office, well, we started digging deeper. Over the last two weeks, we've gathered info on several off-shore accounts. We're talking millions in funds. We were only aware of one until we brought in Hunter."

He hated putting his man in the spotlight. If anyone found out about Hunter returning to his old life even for a good cause, they'd send him back to jail to serve the rest of his time. Among him and his crew, Hunter's involvement was a closely guarded secret.

Everyone started talking at once, and he noticed Ghost picked up Princess, taking her from the room. He'd thank the man later. He clapped his hands to get everyone's attention. Once everyone shut up he turned his head.

"Hunter." Linus held out his hand, Hunter and Wren approached. He wrapped his arm around both of them, hooking his fingers in Wren's belt.

"Thorpe set up a network of safe houses, weigh stations of sorts. Product is delivered and held until it's passed on. Thorpe works as the middleman between supplier and buyer. Powers is the perfect location. A quiet town, small, a lot of the residents work in professions where they travel. I spoke with King."

Everyone looked at the quiet man in the corner. He was a truck driver who spent most of his week out of town.

King didn't step forward. "It's not unheard of to see semis in and out of town, this is a great cut through to avoid the highway on your way to Atlanta. Although, too many new faces and it draws attention.

"A few of the guys I know mentioned that they've been parking out at Thorpe's farm. A favor for a so-called friend. Thorpe set up a good excuse to have trucks out at his place. Trucking is good money, but there's always better, and it ain't unheard of drivers stash a little something extra in their trailers. A few extra pounds here and there gets overlooked at weigh stations."

Linus nodded. "I sent Little out to a do little recon for us. There's a lot of movement out there. He stashed some bugs in the barn. Got in to place a few around the house."

"What about the kids? Thorpe has two sons, Derrick and Craig," Wren asked and drew his attention.

"Derrick is a good kid, off to college in a few months. Craig, Little says he spends a lot of time with a babysitter. I have Little staying close, anything goes down, he has orders to get the kids out."

"Kidnapping—"

He snorted at Wren. "Not kidnapping, a rescue."

He smiled as Wren shook his head and rolled his eyes.

"Could they know about the operation," Crave asked. The big man sat on the floor massaging his man's shoulders. "It could be why they went after Elijah."

Linus could tell Twitch was getting a bit overwhelmed. Twitch was protective of the Brawlers, him and Elijah worked as a team.

"So far, we haven't found any evidence of them knowing about our involvement. If they do, and that's a big if, I hope they wouldn't be stupid enough to go after Scary and Tank's man. That'd be like signing their death warrant."

"Thorpe thinks he's untouchable," Peaches spoke from the doorway.

"He fucking does, he's been a bastard since we were all in school. Rich daddy. Captain of the football team. Motherfucker always thought his shit was golden," Lily shifted on the table.

"She's right. Thorpe keeps everyone in line with fear. He knows everything about everyone," Peaches informed them as she stepped away from the door.

Peaches was the woman to go to when a problem needed to be taken care of legally. Even if some of her methods skirted the law, she knew how to get the job done.

"Should we be pulling in ranks," Scary asked. "We can all head out to Bull's place."

"We should bring Nettie out to the house, Harper too, but she'll probably want to stay at Kyle's place," Twitch spoke up.

Nettie, Crave's mother, needed around the clock care since her ex-husband abused her years ago. Harper was her caretaker, but Harper was too damn delicate to be much help in a fight.

"I'm working from home until I rebuild the office, so, I can keep an eye on Nettie," Gregory offered.

"Can I borrow Psycho for a bit," he asked Scary.

Psycho hadn't attended the meeting to stay with Ben and their kids. Psycho tended to lean toward unpredictable, but he'd called the man in to help a few times over the years.

"He's all yours."

"I don't have any jobs lined up this week, I'm in if you need someone else," Joker said.

"Boss, we definitely need it," Liv said from his spot beside the door.

"Okay, Psycho and you at our office tomorrow. I'll contact Pelter tonight and set up a meeting. We need to stay under the radar on this one. I can't have Hunter at the office, but he can work remote."

"Sin and I can come out to Brawlers to help Twitch behind the bar," Saint quietly spoke.

"That would be great. Without Hunter, this weekend is going to suck," Twitch groaned.

Finally, everyone started talking amongst themselves, and he nudged Wren and Hunter toward the kitchen.

"Do you think it's safe to leave them all alone? They might form a posse to take Thorpe out," Wren asked as he turned and leaned back against the counter.

Wren kept Hunter tucked to his side.

"I hope not. We've put in too many fucking hours to have this operation go south."

He braced his hands against the edge of the counter on either side of them and leaned in.

"Boring evening at work?"

"Too quiet, I stared at the clock more than anything. Did you two have a good day?"

"He made me stay in bed all fucking day and wouldn't even get in with me."

He smiled as Hunter sighed heavily and pouted. Hunter was cute when he was all petulant.

"How dare he," Wren asked.

"We're out of here, boss," Liv spoke behind him.

"Don't call me boss, you only do it to be a dick."

"Would I do that, boss?"

He glanced over his shoulder just in time to catch Liv's smirk. The subtle expression drew attention to the nerve damage Liv suffered from a fire when he was a kid. The man didn't talk about it, and Linus didn't ask. Liv's temper was worse than all of theirs combined.

"Fuck yeah, now clear my house out, I got plans."

"Um, boss, do you think you should exert too much energy, you are—"

"Don't fucking make me get my gun."

"With your aim, you wouldn't hit me."

"Get out."

If Wren or Hunter even thought about laughing they'd get a spanking, he swore. He turned back to his men with his eyes narrowed and glared at them until he heard the commotion in the other room die down.

"Linus, I require affection."

He groaned as he turned and found his mother standing just inside the doorway. The corner of his mouth twitched as she held out her arms and made grabby hands. The snorts and laughter behind him made him growl, which only made his men louder. He strode across the room and wrapped his arms around his mom to lift her off the floor. He buried his face against her neck and inhaled the scent of her favorite incense and the faint odor of weed. Same old Lily.

"Linus, you do what needs to be done to keep our family safe. Just don't die in the process. I'm kinda fond of you."

"I'm kind of fond of you too."

"I love you. Wear your vest and be nice to my future son-in-laws."

"I always wear my vest, and I'm always nice."

"You're higher than I am."

A throat cleared and he knew it was Wren.

"Try to get him to quit his job, I'm really not a fan of his profession."

"I'll see what I can do."

He set her back down.

She reached up and took his face in her hands. "You're still not my favorite."

"And I love Dad more."

He smiled as she cackled and left the room. He was sure she'd hitch a ride to town with Liv. The tiny woman loved the big, awkward man, had since she'd first met Liv.

"Your mother is weird," Wren said, his voice filled with amusement.

Once he was sure she was actually gone, he turned back to his men. "She has her moments."

"I planted the bugs during everyone's dinner break."

Linus knew it was a risk, a huge one on Wren's part. He was humbled by the man's trust in his word. It would make the days and weeks to come easier, especially since he wouldn't have to fight Wren.

"I'll text Little to let him know. Thanks for that."

"I read the file, and what I've seen proves Thorpe has to go."

"Let's get some dinner and relax, I have to be in the office tomorrow." Hunter opened his mouth to argue.

"No, Hunter, I have to go. I don't want Pelter out here. One person catches sight of him, and we're fucked."

"I know, but you're not ready to go out in the field."

He was sore. The incisions and bullet holes healed, stitches and staples were gone, but he knew he wasn't up to par. Hanging back would kill him, but if it kept Hunter happy he'd try.

"If they need me—"

"You'll go, but try to avoid it okay?"

"Okay. Wren get out of the uniform and into comfortable clothes. We'll get dinner together."

"Give me time to shower and change, and I'll be back."

Wren leaned up to kiss Hunter, then pushed away from the counter, he accepted his own before the man disappeared.

Hunter lowered his head and stared down at his bare toes. The uncertainty in his man caused him to frown, and he closed the distance. He grabbed Hunter's waist and leaned down to study Hunter's face.

"What's wrong?"

"I don't want you or Wren to take any risks."

"Hunter, look at me," he paused and waited for Hunter to look at him. "Wren and I have dangerous jobs, it's not going to be easy being with either of us, but for me, I can promise I won't do anything crazy."

Hunter snorted. "You not doing anything crazy is going to be majorly out of character."

"I know, but I have you and Wren, I know it's still early days, but if I can help it, I won't do anything to endanger what I think we got going."

"I'll accept that for now. I better check the casserole Twitch brought over before it burns."

He brought his hands to Hunter's stubble covered cheeks and tilted the man's chin up, then he pressed his mouth to Hunter's. He wanted so much from Hunter and Wren, and even though they hadn't had the talk, he wanted these men. This wasn't some one-off for him. He just hoped he could make it work and he'd do everything within his power not to fuck it up.

He deepened the kiss, then eased it as he drew back.

"Check on dinner, and I'll go lock up."

Hunter gave him a small smile, and he let Hunter go. He couldn't take his eyes off the taller man. He'd waited so long to have him. He liked Hunter and Wren in his house, he'd keep them there as long as he could. As soon as he got Thorpe off everyone's ass, then he'd focus on his men and claim them if they'd put up with him.

15 THIS SADLY WASN'T HUNTER'S HOME

Hunter's fingers flew over the keys, and he only paused long enough to take quick sips of his coffee. Linus had slipped from bed before the sun even came up. He hadn't wanted Linus to go. Linus had gotten maybe two hours of sleep. The three of them had spent most of the night in bed, talking between kisses and flirting. It was nice. He hadn't imagined he'd have one man in his life much less two, but he did have them.

They'd shared stories of growing up, Linus' stories a lot more humorous than his and Wren's, but they'd laughed and relaxed. Linus and Wren took every opportunity to kiss and hug him. He liked it too much and feared losing it. That it would be there one minute and gone the next. So he cherished each one and didn't dare to hope for more.

He'd also become too used to being there in Linus' home. It wasn't his even though he'd started to feel more comfortable there than at the farm.

Shit, he wasn't focusing, he put his mind back on his work. Hours passed since he'd started the search. What he did wasn't always illegal, but he did have a knack for research, and he liked it. He loved his job at Brawlers, but this, this job he did for Linus was what he wanted to do.

He jolted as firm lips pushed the side of his neck. He'd twisted his hair up before he'd started work.

"Good afternoon, why didn't you wake me?"

"You needed sleep, you didn't get much yesterday before you had to go to work, and we talked most of the night. I let you sleep in."

"What time did Linus take off?"

"About five. Pelter was going to be at the office at six."

"Find anything interesting," Wren asked.

Strong hands pushed beneath the t-shirt he'd swiped from Linus. Fingers sunk into the slight softness of his stomach and he tried to suck it in.

"Don't do that, baby."

"Do what?"

"Don't try to act stupid, I know you're not."

Wren sucked at the spot behind his ear and stroked his hands upward. Wren pinched at his nipples, and he leaned back in his chair and arched into the rough pressure.

"I was hoping to wake up with you still in bed. Can you take a break?"

"Ye...yes."

Disappointment overtook him as Wren's touch and warmth disappeared.

"Stand up and turn to face me."

He did as Wren said and turned to find Wren wearing nothing but a pair of Linus' pajama bottoms. He grinned as he realized him and Wren wore more of Linus' clothes than Linus did.

"What are you smiling about?"

"I was just thinking we wear Linus' clothes more than he does."

"Probably true. Are you still okay with this, us?"

Oddly Wren seemed suddenly insecure. He knew they hadn't really talked about what it was between them, but he'd felt they were all on the same page.

"Yes, what about you?"

Wren stepped toward him and wrapped his arms around his waist, "Yes, but I can't get a read on Linus."

"That's not unusual. Linus is a bit hard to figure out."

"What have you figured out, I'm the newbie in the relationship."

Wren's hands moved beneath his shirt again and stroked up and down his back, pulling him closer each pass.

"He's a loner." He kissed Wren. "He's fearless." He pressed his lips to one corner of Wren's mouth and then the other. "He's strangely sweet."

"Then why didn't you make a move on him first?"

Hunter dropped his head back and stared up at the ceiling. Wren stroked his tongue up his throat.

"Have you seen him?"

"Yes, but that's not an answer."

"He's gorgeous and capable, intelligent. Loyal. Honest. He's like the perfect package even with his asshole tendencies, but I think it's just the—"

Wren nipped and sucked at the side of his neck. His cock pushed at the soft cotton of his sleep pants. Wren started to push his shirt up, he only hesitated a second before he lifted his arms and let Wren remove it.

The way Wren stared at him made every inch of him ache. The desire in Wren's eyes was more than he had ever dreamed of seeing when someone looked at him. Wren was muscular and compact, his skin smooth and tanned.

"Fuck, it's like I won the boyfriend lottery." Wren leaned in to stroke one cheek then the other over his chest. "Two hairy men that are all mine."

His entire body jerked when Wren's tongue flicked over his nipple. His nipples were always super sensitive. He laid his arms over Wren's broad shoulders and combed his fingers through Wren's hair, leading the man closer to his chest. He arched as Wren wrapped his lips around his nipple and sucked hard enough to cause a bite of pain. His eyelids fluttered closed and then flew open as he felt Wren fall to his knees.

His pants were tugged down to the middle of his thighs, and Wren swallowed him to the root. He locked his knees as he felt his legs start to give out. Wren groaned and hummed around his cock, his pace quick and the pressure just right. He curled his toes into the thick carpet. Thick hands gripped his cheeks and pulled them apart while fingertips dipped into his crease. Massaged his clenching hole and pushed, the tips of two fingers slipped passed the tight muscle.

The sight of his dick quickly disappearing and reappearing as Wren bobbed along his length quicker and rougher was too much.

He bowed his back as he curved over Wren and tried to hold onto control. He clawed at Wren's broad back with his short nails. He felt the head of his cock slip into Wren's throat, and the man swallowed, once, twice and a third time before pulling back.

Hard, brutal hands spun him and pushed at his lower back until he bent over to place his hands one dining room table. Wren parted his ass, and warm breath moved over him, a tongue swiped slowly over his hole, then sucked.

He dropped his forehead to the cool surface of the table and arched his hips up, pushed back into the prod of Wren's tongue. He stretched his arms out to grab the opposite side of the table. Wren tongue-fucked his ass in shallow thrusts. The whimpers slipping from his mouth made his face heat in embarrassment. He sounded needy.

The urge to beg for more overtook him but then Wren's index and middle fingers prodded at his hole. Wren spit and spread it, pushing at his muscle until it gave and the burn had him shifting his feet farther apart.

He pushed out, and Wren's fingers pushed deeper, clenching around them.

"Wren, please, I need—"

"I know what my man needs."

Wren's breath fanned his hole, and then the warmth of Wren's breath and touch disappeared. He jerked his head up and peeked over his shoulder to find Wren standing behind him. The man's gaze locked on his ass and he started to straighten so to cover himself.

"No, you're so sexy. I thought so the first time I saw you. It was months ago. You were sitting on your bike. Glasses perched on your nose as you typed away on your phone. You were frowning." Wren's rough hands stroked up his back. "I wanted to kiss it away."

"You did?" he asked as he laid his cheek on the table.

"Oh yeah, catching sight of you every night was the highlight of my shift."

A small smile pulled at the corners of his mouth. He shivered as cool lube trickled down his crease and Wren worked his hole with his fingertips, slowly stretching him until Wren fucked him with three broad fingers. He rode them as Wren blanketed his back, whispered about all the things Wren wanted to do to him.

"Do you want me to fuck you right here, bent over the table," Wren asked.

"Yes, please, Wren, I'll beg."

"Baby, you never have to beg me to love you."

Wren's body shifted behind him, and his fingers disappeared. He faintly heard the crinkle of a condom wrapper. He held his breath as he waited for the first push of Wren's cock into him. The stretch and the burn, the fullness, and the love. He clawed at the smooth tabletop at the first tender push.

He waited for it to be like the times before—the men before—the ones who took him without care or tenderness. The men who used him, but they hadn't been Wren or Linus. They'd never treated him with anything other than respect and gentleness. They kissed and touched him without expectations.

Tears burned at his eyes and slipped from beneath his lids as Wren loved him with gentle thrusts and shallow grinds. Wren gruffly spoke against his ear, telling him he was beautiful. How much Wren wanted him.

Wren's left hand rested over his lacing their fingers together. His man slipped his other arm around him and gripped his cock, squeezed him tightly as Wren stroked him in time with his slow rhythm. He gripped Wren's hand as he felt his balls draw up and his toes curled into the carpet.

He clenched his teeth as he groaned as his cock pulsed and he came. Wren's movements faltered and then his man ground against his ass. Wren's teeth sunk into his shoulder as he felt the heat and pulse as his man came.

"Mine, always mine," Wren said quietly between kisses.

Wren's mouth brushed his cheek that was damp from sweat and tears. He turned his head until Wren's mouth settled on his and they shared an unhurried kiss. He kept his eyes closed to disguise his tears. He needed this to last. To savor what he hoped love felt like.

16 WHO VOLUNTEERED HIM FOR A STAKEOUT? OH YEAH, LINUS

Wren must have been a serial killer in a previously life because that's the only reason he'd be stuck with Little and Joker in a cramped surveillance van. Linus was going to pay for this one. Why couldn't they have put him with Ghost? The man was an absolute sweetheart and sane, main thing Ghost was sane.

The other two men were having a glaring contest. Little had cracked jokes since they'd gotten into the van two hours ago and drove out to the outskirts of Thorpe's farm.

He should've known better when Linus asked him for a favor.

Little was relaxed into a threadbare recliner with his ankles crossed like it was just any other day. Joker was in the opposite corner pretending to read a book. He grabbed his phone from the console that held all of Little's monitors and gadgets. He unlocked his phone and pulled up the message thread between him, Hunter, and Linus. They shared separate texts between them, but the one they used most was the one between all three of them.

Wren: *I'm going to kill you for this.*

Hunter: *What did I do?*

Wren: *NOT YOU!*

Hunter: *Why is Linus laughing? It's scary.*

Wren snorted loudly and glanced around to find Joker and Little staring at him.

"Boyfriends," Little asked.

"Yeah."

It was still weird everyone seemed to accept the three of them without batting a lash. It shouldn't have been though, Scary, Elijah, and Tank made it look easy. Over the last month, he'd spent a lot of time with the Crews, and it was surreal. He had never met a tighter group of friends or relationships as strong. He would admit before he'd met the Crews and he had only observed from the shadows that he was jealous.

"Linus is solid. He's the dude to have in your corner."

Joker grunted in what he assumed was an affirmation. The man didn't talk much. He'd heard plenty of rumors around town about Joker's past. Even if half of it were true, then Joker had walked through Hell without a lot of sanity left.

"Figured that out pretty quick. He did send y'all out to take multiple bullets for his team."

"Ah, that's nothing, ask him about the time he almost lost a kidney when a jumper tried to knife me in the back. Linus didn't go down until he had the fucker in cuffs."

Great, another Linus almost died story, he was hearing too many of them. The man needed a keeper.

His phone beeped.

Linus: *Not having fun?*
Wren: *I'm waiting for them to attack each other.*
Linus: *Prelude to porno?*
Wren grimaced.
Wren: *I hope the hell not!*
Linus: *That would be an anger bang for the ages.*
Hunter: *I don't wanna see Little's naked ass!*
Wren: *I don't either. Don't expect a yes the next time you ask me for a favor.*
Linus: *Is Little and Joker reeking of weed and incense?*
Wren: *Not my business!*

Of course, his boyfriends would belong to a Crew where things like laws were bendable or easily ignored. He was going to have to learn to ignore more than half of what his new friends and family said or did.

His phone chimed, and he opened the media message to find a picture of Linus and Hunter spooning on the couch shirtless and smiling. He smiled and did the stupidest thing he had ever done, he stroked the screen with his thumb. They'd spent every free minute together since Linus came home from the hospital. It was odd to be away from them.

Hot breath fanned his neck and swore he was a deep breath away from a contact high. He swatted Little away, and then Joker looked over his other shoulder.

"You got a thing for Furries, man, because that's a lot of fucking hair. Total hairball waiting to happen, shit," Little said and shook his head, the man's unkempt beard brushed his neck.

He leaned to the side to get away only to bump Joker's cheek.

"Personal space, bastards."

"Dude, you got two men, ain't nothing personal about your…space."

Great, now Joker had jokes…and bad ones at that.

"Aren't you two supposed to be watching the monitors?"

"Don't want to share sexting with the boyfriends, come on, be a friend, neither of us is getting any, we live vicariously through everyone else."

He cracked a smile at Little's pouting. The rumors were Little got more than the whole Crew's share of partners. Joker didn't even look at anyone unless it was to scowl or threaten violence.

"Well, you're not living vicariously through me."

With all the shit going down with Thorpe and everything else, him and his men hadn't had a lot of time for the sex part of their relationship. It might sound strange, but he liked that even at the beginning it wasn't reduced to just sex.

They grumbled and moved back to their respective posts.

Wren: *You're going to pay for this.*

He hit send and set his phone aside, when it beeped twice he ignored it and stared at the monitors. Lights illuminated the infrared cameras.

"We got movement," he said.

Little bounced out of his recliner and bent over, his fingers flying over the keyboard, then used the joystick to zoom in. Three semis pulled up to one of the three barns and parked. A Kevlar vest slapped him on the chest, and he turned his head to look at Joker.

"Wear it."

The order in Joker's voice was clear, and he wasn't going to argue. He slipped it over his head and secured the Velcro straps.

"Shit, eight of them, all heavily armed. Boss, you read me?"

Linus' voice came over the earpiece Little shoved at him earlier.

"Go head."

"Sound a little breathless there, boss."

"Head in the game, Little, or I'll hide your van."

"No need to be mean."

"What's the situation?"

"Eight heavily armed men, Thorpe and Cabot are on site—"

"I think it's about to get ugly," he said.

One of the new arrivals was in the lead and by his body language, he was the man in charge. Thorpe was in the man's face. Cabot had his hand on his sidearm as Thorpe gesticulated wildly.

"Standby, boss."

He watched Little's usual mischievous expression disappear as the man studied the situation. The swiftness of the change made him do a double-take.

"Boss, permission to go with the retrieval mission?"

Retrieval mission—that didn't sound good or legal. It's a good thing he didn't particularly like his job. He knew Linus was short staffed, maybe he could get a job after he got out of prison. Linus already hired the least law-abiding Crew. He'd fit right in.

"You're good to go, but if my man even gets a scratch, you're dead."

"You can kiss all his boo-boos when he gets home."

"Do as I say, or your van takes a trip to the scrapyard."

"Don't threaten my baby!"

"Then you better keep him safe, or your body will still be in the van when I crush it."

Wren couldn't help his smile at Linus threatening to kill someone over him. He shook his head as he realized what he'd thought. Yeah, he fitted in too well.

"I hear ya loud and clear."

"Wren, keep your head down, wear your fucking vest, and don't disobey me or I'll redden your fucking ass so quick you won't know what fucking happened. Understand?"

"Linus, quit threatening Wren."

Wren laughed at Hunter's chiding tone.

"Let's get this over with so I can get home to my men," he announced.

"Damn right, everyone stay in contact at all times. I want check-ins every five minutes. Retrieval should be an in and out OP. I'll have a safe house arranged in thirty. Got it?"

There was something damn sexy about the authority in Linus' voice. This wasn't the time for a hard-on especially when he was sure in a few minutes he'd break several laws.

"Got it," they all answered.

Little crouched down. "This is what we're going to do. Joker, I need your eyes on Thorpe at all times. Alert us to any movement. Wren, you're going to be on my six. I disabled the motion sensors on the south side of the house. We stick to the shadows. We go quick. We go quiet. You stay on my heels."

"I've done raids a time or two, Little."

"I'm sure, but this isn't official."

Little lifted his arm and killed the lights, then checked his weapon. He heard the click of the safety and the smooth slide of metal against metal as Little chambered the first round.

The van door slid open and let in the dim moonlight. He followed Little and was amazed how silent the normally loquacious, brute could be when he was on point. He pulled his gun from his holster and deftly held it in his hands. He stayed on the burly man's heels, checking his six as they made their way through a thick tree line.

A large two-story farmhouse came into view.

"Check in," Linus' gruff voice filled his head.

"House in sight," Little answered.

Joker snorted and then spoke up, "Thorpe's asking for an ass whooping."

"As long as he's distracted," he said.

"We're going silent."

They quietly jogged across the yard and when they reached it, turned and pressed their backs to the siding.

"Derrick and Craig's rooms are on the first floor," Little whispered.

He nodded, and they hugged the wall until they reached a dimly lit window. He watched Little peek into the window. He nearly punched Little when the man tapped on the window.

"What the—"

The window creaked as it was opened. "Little? What are you doing here?"

A shot rang out, someone screamed, and men bellowed. The skinny boy with the small voice widened his eyes. The boy froze.

"Hey, Derrick. I need you to get Craig."

"What's going—"

"I'll explain later, we got no time now. Get your ass moving."

From that moment, chaos reigned. Hours seemed to pass as they waited for Derrick to reappear. A chunky bundle was lifted out of the window. He holstered his weapon as he was suddenly in possession of a sleeping toddler. Little helped Derrick to the ground.

"Derrick, you're going to be on me, keep your fingers in my belt loop and don't look back. Wren has Craig."

He waited for the teenager to lose his shit, but all the boy did was nod. They headed deeper into the shadows, and the trip was a little longer getting back to the van.

More shouting and cursing echoed through the silence of the night, and he chanced a look to find that whatever happened was breaking up. Thorpe was on his ass in the dirt. Cabot had his gun trained on the guy who seemed to be in charge.

"Joker, we're two minutes out.'"

Tiny whimpers drew his attention to the baby powder scented bundle in his arms, and he adjusted the kid. He breathed a sigh of relief as the faint outline of the black van came into view, and the door slid open. Joker grabbed Derrick's arm and tugged him inside. The man tried to take Craig.

"I got him. Let's get out of here."

Little was already in the driver's seat. Derrick was curled into a ball behind it. The faint light of the monitors highlighted terrified features.

"Boss, we're out. Where we headed?"

"The office, we'll arrange transport when y'all get there."

He didn't know how sound of an idea that was, but he wasn't going to question it. Their luck held out so far;

he hoped it continued to do so. When they were far enough away, he reached up to turn on the dim overhead light. He lowered his hand to push the blanket away from the toddler's face. Anger stole through him at the hand print bruise on the cute, chubby cheek.

"Craig has an ear infection, and he wouldn't stop crying. Dad didn't like it."

He turned his head to stare at Derrick and noticed the fingertip black and blue marks just showing from under his short sleeves. The kid was almost delicate and didn't look like he had enough meals. He faintly remembered seeing the kid around town, but nothing more than that.

"You hungry?"

Derrick's pale face turned red, and he answered, "Yes, sir."

"Name's Wren. When we get home, I'll see what we have. Did you bring medicine or anything for Craig?"

"I packed a quick bag and made sure it was in there."

"Okay, just lay your head back, and we'll be somewhere safe soon, okay?"

Derrick simply nodded and closed his eyes.

He placed his hand on Craig's forehead and pushed back the baby's soft blond hair. Craig had the cutest little button nose and chubbiest cheeks he'd ever seen. He hadn't spent much time around children, but this had to be the cutest one.

He'd worry about the fact he'd become an accessory to kidnapping later. Getting the kids safe was more important. He was going to need to find a new job after this.

17 LET'S JUST CALL IT A RESCUE, SHALL WE?

Linus perched on the edge of the long table and crossed his arms over his chest. Shit going south on his operations was becoming a habit he didn't have time for. They'd had a plan in place in the event the Thorpe kids needed to be grabbed. Derrick was seventeen, plenty old enough to take Craig out for the night. That still wasn't looking like it was going to save their asses though.

"It was a rescue mission, and that's all you need to know." He looked across the conference room at a pissed off and pacing Pelter.

"It was a kidnapping, Linus. What the fuck were you thinking?"

"I was thinking there were gunshots and innocents in the vicinity. We made a choice, and I stand behind my team's decision."

"Of course, you would. Little is going to end up in a cell one of these days."

"Not going to happen, I got the best lawyer in the country on retainer."

"Peaches, you have Peaches on retainer, that woman—"

"I wouldn't complain about her. Last I heard, her friends don't like—"

"Stop right there. Why did I even ask you to help me with this?"

"Because you're a moron who had no other choice. You don't like how I run my missions then you can take a fucking walk."

Pelter lifted his hands and rubbed his palms over the stubble on his scalp. The man seemed to have aged overnight. Corruption wasn't the easiest racket, especially when the cases typically involved perps with badges. Pelter was in his mid-forties but looked older.

"You and your team are killing me. Nothing we can do about it now. I can't take them, Linus."

"What do you mean you can't take them? We discussed this shit, we get witnesses you put them in protective custody."

"We have a seventeen-year-old frightened kid whose suffered unknown years of abuse and a three-year-old who can't testify. Also, are we forgetting the fact you kidnapped them?"

"Derrick got scared and ran away with his brother when he heard gunshots and commotion."

"Bullshit, Linus, this was supposed to be off the books. This was a recon OP only."

"What the fuck am I supposed to do with them?"

"You're going to protect them. Protection Services is one of your specialties."

"Shit, you do know I have two men at home. I already got to watch them because one's employed by the Powers Sheriff Department and the other is a convicted felon who Thorpe would cum in his jeans just to bust."

"Not my problem. You let Little out there without a leash. This is on you."

"Fuck," he growled.

His brain started working overtime. He couldn't involve Gage, and he'd kept the man as far away from this as he could. He was the only one who could spin whatever fucked up mess they got themselves in, into a plausible story. Little couldn't be trusted to make one sane decision. Liv and Pure were already stretched too thin gathering evidence. He was the only option. What the hell was he going to do with kids in his house? He cussed like a fucking sailor, and he had two men he slept with every night.

"We're so close to taking Thorpe down, man, I can't take chances."

"I get that, I do, but—"

"Just a little longer, I just need more time to make a case that'll stand up."

"Okay, let me talk to Wren and see what we can come up with."

"I'll contact you in a few days."

"Check out small practices and vet clinics, we may have wounded, and that could give us a name."

"I'll get on it when I get back to the office."

It was all Pelter said before he was gone and left him alone in the room. A door opening pulled his attention away from plans. Wren walked in, and he couldn't help but smile. The man hadn't put that kid down since they got to the office an hour ago.

"Come here," he said.

"So, it didn't sound like things went well," Wren spoke as he made his way to him.

He grabbed the man's hips and pulled Wren between his thighs. He tilted his head to study the bruising on Craig's cheek. He raised his left hand to stroke along the bluish-purple mark.

"They're going to stay out at our place for a few days until we can figure this shit out."

"Good, I didn't really feel comfortable letting them go somewhere else."

The sad little smile on Wren's mouth pained him. He'd quickly learned he didn't like Wren unhappy any more than he did Hunter. That didn't bode well for the future if he couldn't tell his men no and they'd only technically been together a month since he got out of the hospital.

"Little eats like he's sixteen so we'll talk to Derrick and see what they need food wise. Clothes, we might have to head out of town for that. Until then, one more person stealing my clothes shouldn't be a problem."

Craig sniffled in his sleep and raised his hand to rub at his tiny ear. Wren, as if on auto-pilot, rubbed Craig's back to sooth him.

Oh shit, this wasn't going to be good. He didn't do the whole former parasites running around his house thing. His nephew was a weird little shit, so he dealt with it.

"Don't get too—"

"Too late, so let's get everything set up so we can get the kids home. It's almost midnight and Hunter will be home in a few hours. I don't like him coming into an empty house."

Wren leaned in to give him a quick kiss, but he wasn't going to let that go. He wrapped his hand around the back of Wren's neck and pulled his mouth tighter against his. Wren moaned, and he thrust his tongue passed the man's lips. It wasn't the time, but he'd worried about Wren. He'd known Little and Joker would watch his man's back, but it wasn't him doing it. He softened the kiss and brushed gentle caresses to the firm curves.

"It'll be fine."

Wren nodded. "I'll go get a list from Derrick while you take care of whatever it is you do."

He watched every move Wren made until the man exited the opened door. He reached for his phone and called the only person he could think of. The phone rang a few times before it connected.

"Hey, Ma, I need to talk."

"Do I have grandkids?"

"You know way too fucking much for not working for me."

"Little called."

He heard the amusement in her voice and promised to take his snitch of an employee out later.

"You have to stop bribing my guys."

"Little came to keep me company earlier."

"Dad approve of your new bestie?"

"Not particularly, not Damon's type."

Linus snorted loud as he listened to his mother laugh. It was a musical and happy sound, they might have had their differences over the years, but no one could ask for a more loving mother aside from Peaches.

"I can see it in his eyes, Ma."

"You'll be fine, and just think, you're way past the newborn stage. After two it's pretty much smooth sailing. If not, you can always visit me."

"What do I know—"

"You listen to me, Linus Peace Trenton, I may not have been the best or sanest mother around, but I love each and every one of you fucked up spawns. I know life wasn't easy with me as your mother, but I wanted y'all to know that nothing you ever did or said would make me love y'all less. You grew up strong in spite of being considered weird.

"You have this amazing chance with two great men, and if, and I mean if because I know you, you let your men love you it's the most amazing thing in the world. I just want my three spawns to know what it's like to be loved like your father loves me. To know an acceptance that has no limits, no strings."

"I know, Ma."

He'd grown up witnessing that almost symbiotic exchange between his parents. They were so attuned to each other they instantly sensed what the other needed. His dad put Lily first. She got the first plate of food after his dad fed them. Five minutes didn't pass with them in the same room without his parents touching, even something as simple as a brush of hands as they walked past each other.

In some secret part of him, he'd always wanted that. That unquestioning acceptance of flaws and perfections in equal parts.

"I know your job is dangerous, Linus, and I want you to wear your vest, keep a trusted comrade at your six, and make sure you come home to your men. Promise?"

"I promise."

"Okay, it's late, and you're still at the office, get Wren and the kids home. If you need clothes or whatever call."

"I will."

"I love you, Linus."

"Love you too, Ma."

He disconnected the call, slid off the table and went to find Wren so he could get them home. He was like Wren, he didn't like Hunter coming home to an empty house. Everything would work itself out. He just hoped they were all in one piece when it did.

18 WHO WAS THE LITTLE PERSON HIDING IN THE CLOSET?

Hunter opened the front door at almost three a.m., he should've been home an hour ago. He was exhausted. He spent all day searching for anything to bring Thorpe down, grabbed a nap, then headed to Brawlers for work. He was missing his men. Hopefully, they were both home, and he could actually go to sleep snuggled up between them.

He slipped off his backpack and set it beside the door. It was still odd to come home to a quiet house. He hadn't realized how used to the chaos of Brawlers Farm he'd become.

"Hey, you're home." Wren peeked out of the kitchen doorway. "You're late, but we kept dinner warm for you."

"Thanks, I'm sorry." He strode across the room and wrapped his arms around Wren.

"No need to be sorry," Wren said against his mouth.

Wren's hands combed through his hair, and he leaned his head back into the touch. Wren's fingertips massaged his scalp. Goosebumps spread over his skin. The kiss they shared was slow and tender, no rush to the end. It was nothing like the ones he'd experienced before as few as they were.

"Where's Linus?"

Strong hands stroked up and down his back. He loved when Wren and Linus touched him. He'd spent so many years alone and the rest just trying to survive. When he'd moved there, he'd found the family he always wanted, and he hadn't visited his parents over the past year.

"Shower, he just got back from a run. Why don't you go join him, and I'll heat everything back up?"

"You sure?"

"Hunter, this is the three of us, but I have no illusions we won't get on each other's nerves from time to time. I love all three of us spending time together, but also, I want us to spend one-on-one time together."

"I know, I'm just tired."

When he started to step back, Wren smacked his ass, and he rolled his eyes.

"Then do as I say."

"Just because Linus is the boss—"

"Linus isn't the boss," Wren muttered.

"He so is, you just don't want to admit it."

Wren's broad frame pressed him back against the frame. His man slipped his hands beneath his shirt and stroked over the curve of his stomach, pushed slightly into the softness. He didn't even try to suck in his stomach to flatten it. Wren's eyes locked with his and were filled with heat and desire.

He pushed his hands between them and placed his hands flat against Wren's powerful chest as he felt the muscles flex under his hands.

"Do you know how beautiful you are," Wren asked. Wren's fingertips stroked over his face.

"Not beaut—"

Wren cut off his objection with a rough kiss. Wren's hard angles conformed to his softer body. He loved the muscularity of Wren and Linus, and he'd memorized every scar. The places he could touch that made them catch their breath.

Wren possessed his mouth, clutched at him and touched wherever he could reach. He moaned as he lifted his right leg to wrap around Wren's thick thigh.

"Shit," a strange voice had him pushing Wren away.

"Who's that," Hunter asked as he stared at the skinny teenager frozen in the middle of their living room. Fuck, not theirs, Linus', this wasn't his house.

"Oh, damn, that's Derrick, he's crashing here for a few days. We hope you don't mind," Wren blushed and smiled sheepishly, "I kind of forgot when I saw you."

"Hi, Derrick." He kept his body pressed to Wren's.

What the hell was Thorpe's son doing there?

"Hi. I'm sorry, I didn't mean to—"

"You're fine, I'm going to go find Linus and say hi. I just got home from work."

"Come on, Derrick, you hungry," Wren asked.

"A little, but I don't want to be a bother."

"You're not a bother," he spoke up before Wren could. He hated the way the boy's shoulders slumped as if he were trying to make himself as small as possible. It reminded him too much of himself. "Feed him."

"On it." Wren gave him a quick kiss. "Now who's trying to be all bossy?" Wren laughed and ducked into the kitchen.

"I'm sorry I didn't mean to interrupt."

"It's okay, really, I'm going to go find Linus."

"Okay, thank you."

Derrick quickly passed him and went into the kitchen. Okay, so they had another person in the house since he'd left for work. He walked toward the bedrooms, and into Linus' room that they shared. The bed was not big enough for the three of them, but he liked Wren and Linus sleeping close to him.

He crossed the room to the closet and opened it, He saw tiny chubby feet peeking from a pile of blankets on the floor.

"About time you got home," Linus grumped.

He turned to find Linus in nothing but a towel around his hips.

"Is there a reason we have a little person in our closet?"

"I put his little ass into bed like fucking twice."

He tried to hide his smile as Linus huffed and strode toward him, warm skin dotted with beads of water pressed against his back. Strong arms circled his waist. Linus' beard tickled the side of this neck.

"We have temporary roommates."

"Maybe, Wren wants to keep one of them."

"The one in the closet?"

"Yeah, that one."

"And?"

"He looked so cute with it."

His cheeks ached from the wide smile that pulled at the corners of his mouth, and he chuckled at the feigned disgust in Linus' voice. He'd studied the man far too long not to realize when Linus pretended to be cranky. He lifted his arm and reached back to rub Linus' short, wet hair.

"It probably has a name."

After seeing Derrick downstairs and seeing plenty of files over the months, he knew exactly who they were.

"Craig."

"Why are the Thorpe kids here?"

"You know what happened, but I'll fill you in again on what happened after you left for work. Wren, Joker and Little—"

"The story already sounds like a clusterfuck."

"As you know, the deal went bad out there while they were observing, and I gave the go-ahead on the retrieval—"

"Kidnapping—"

He stifled a laugh at Linus' disgruntled expression. Kidnappings were always called retrieval missions. Even all the Jumpers they'd gone after who were bound and gagged in the trunk of one vehicle or another were never referred to as what they were. Linus was the worst of them. He got the most amusement out of planning the kid—retrieval missions.

"Retrieval, we're moving on, Pelter said he'd put witnesses in protective custody. But since me and the guys are working in an unofficial capacity, we're on the hook for protection detail."

"Is he going to sleep in our closet all night?"

"No, I got it."

"It has a name."

"Whatever," Linus grumbled and placed a loud kiss on his throat.

"Take the blankets with you, he might like them."

"Good idea."

Linus crouched down and picked up the pile of blankets with the toddler sandwiched between the layers.

The chubby cheeks, cupid bow lips—the boy was adorable, then he noticed something.

"Wait," "he sharply ordered.

Linus stopped, and he lifted the blanket. A perfect hand print bruise marred the peaches and cream complexion.

"What happened?"

"It wasn't us."

"I didn't think it was."

"Derrick said Craig has an ear infection, he was crying and Thorpe didn't like it."

"He's not going back."

"I promise, he won't."

"Maybe we can bring Matty over today for a play date. I'm off so I can watch them."

"Call Lucky or Priest and set it up. I have to go into town to pick up some clothes for Derrick, he didn't bring any of his stuff only Craig's."

"He didn't bring anything?"

"Hey, look at me," Linus ordered. "He's fine, he has what he needs and what he doesn't we can get him."

"But he shouldn't have to do without until—"

"He has his backpack with all his school books and his laptop. He said he can miss a few days of school, but his college courses he can't, and he does those online. Wren and I will get him to make a list. It'll be taken care of."

"I'm sorry."

"Don't be sorry. You're sweet and caring, only a few reasons why I love you. Now, I'm taking the heathen back to the guest room. He better stay this time."

Linus left like he hadn't just tipped his world on its side. Love, Linus said he loved him. Maybe it was just a figure of speech. Qualities that Linus loved about him, not

156

him *him* like he wished. He roughly shook his head, reached into the closet and pulled down whatever, then headed for the bathroom. He should've been ecstatic, but he felt let down and depressed. His brain dissecting each word or action Linus made over the years. Did Linus feel the same as him or was he projecting?

He sighed sadly. He stripped and stepped into the still steamy glass, shower stall. He turned around until the scalding spray cascaded down his back and he bit back the tears that he stupidly allowed to fall. Although it was okay, no one ever knew the tears he shed because he only allowed his moments of weakness when he knew no one was around who could see or care.

19 SO MUCH FOR BROTHERHOOD IN BLUE OR WHATEVER

The Sheriff Station was packed with all hands-on deck which was odd at almost 2 a.m. The uncomfortable tension oppressive, but not one mention of Sheriff Thorpe's missing children came up. The fact Thorpe wasn't sending out every man he had to search for his kids pissed him off. If they were his, criminal or not, he'd be out there until he found them.

When he'd left the house earlier, Derrick had barely acknowledged his presence as the teenager studied. Derrick mumbled about a paper due. Hunter had Matty and Craig at the table having dinner. His man looked good with kids in the house. Hunter attentive to their needs and moods, Craig perched on Hunter's hip.

Linus had even played with Matty and Craig, not for long, but the man was almost humorously uncomfortable around what the man referred to as former parasites.

He'd fallen hard for his men, Linus and Hunter were the perfect man in two bodies. He wanted more, yet there seemed to be something off with Hunter that morning. Hunter shied away from affection from Linus and him. He didn't like when Hunter pulled away. It was as if they were back to the day he'd asked Hunter out. They hadn't had a lot of time to talk. Everything seemed to be working against them when it came to spending alone time together.

Yes, they slept in the same bed, talked and shared stories about themselves, but they hadn't set in stone what they wanted from a relationship between them. He wanted it all, them as a family, the three of them and maybe if he was lucky—he ended the thought before it formed. Wishing for what was surely impossible wouldn't do anything but break his heart in the end.

Whispers in harsh tones caught his attention, and he jerked his head up from the report he'd been pretending to read. Thorpe, Cabot, and another older Deputy named Post were headed for the door. He made sure no one was paying attention to him, and he stood, slipped out the back way. He hugged the exterior wall and stayed to the shadows as he made his way around to the front.

He only caught pieces of the conversation but enough to tell him whatever was going on wouldn't end without bloodshed. Brawlers was mentioned. Last call. He wanted to think Thorpe wasn't crazy enough to try to take down the Brawlers Crew on his own with only a few Deputies as back up.

He brought his arm back to slip his phone from his back pocket. He quickly swiped to unlock his phone and dialed Linus' number.

"Trenton."

"Linus, call Scary and Tank, I think Thorpe and Cabot are headed that way."

"Would they even be fucking—"

"I think they'd be that crazy. You know Scary and Tank, the rest of their Crew are already out for blood with what happened with Elijah."

"Fuck, the Executioners are there tonight. How quick can you get there?"

"I'll give them a few minutes head start, and then I'm following."

"Stay down, make sure you have your vest. I already sent a 9-1-1 to my team. I'll call Scary and Tank, then get a hold of Pelter. We need to be official."

"Put your vest on and no heroics, got me?"

"Whatever you say."

"Linus, don't—"

The call disconnected, and he huffed.

"Bastard," he growled as he shoved his phone back into his pocket.

Thorpe's cruiser and a second disappeared around the corner at the end of the block. He jogged quickly to his *Jeep*. He started it and started the pursuit.

He was glad he didn't like his job and needed a new one. He wouldn't be standing shoulder to shoulder with his fellow Deputies. His men and family were in danger, that took all precedents. He slowed a bit on the way out of town until he kept the taillights in front of him just within view.

He wanted to call to check on the plan, but he knew Linus and his Crew were prepared for whatever. So, he was just concerned for the Brawlers Crew. Saturdays were normally all hands-on since Elijah normally came in, along with the Twirled Crews, and a lot of the husbands.

The time he'd spent around the Crews, he knew they were capable of handling their own. It was one thing to skirt the law and another to go head-to-head, which for the past few years he'd seen an escalation. Especially with Peaches in their corner.

Brawlers was only a few miles ahead. He didn't attempt to disguise the fact he was following Thorpe. He was only a few minutes behind, yet when he pulled into the parking lot guns were already drawn.

"Where's my kids," Thorpe bellowed as he waved him gun around the crowd.

It was just like he feared, everyone was there. He rushed from the vehicle already pulling his service weapon.

"Motherfucker, we saw what you did and there ain't no way you're getting that boy back," Joker hissed between clenched teeth as he tried to push his way between Scary and Tank.

"Thorpe," Peaches calmly stepped into the line of fire.

Gib called her name, but he shut up when she lifted her arm and silenced the dissension behind her. He caught Linus' gaze as he made his way to stand behind Peaches.

"You're not going to solve anything this way. Put your weapons—"

"Shut the fuck up, bitch."

Thorpe made a mistake because everyone started to converge. Gib was the only one to break the line and step up beside Peaches.

"You'll show my wife some respect. We've put up with your bigotry and your outright assault on our boys, but that shit ends now. We've contacted the authorities about Craig, and I'm sure Derrick will be forthcoming about outlining all the abuse you've put those two boys through."

"Assault, you're a bunch of deviants, and Derrick is no different, who'd take your fucking word for shit?"

"I would," Pelter answered as he stepped up. "We have enough evidence to arrest you for Human trafficking, drug trafficking and corruption. The list goes on, we've already frozen your accounts and filed for warrants."

The man was decked out in tactical gear. The coldness in the man's dark green eyes made a shiver work down his spine.

He stayed to the side and took it all in, waiting for the moment it went from calm to chaos. He had no doubt it would. Cabot and Post moved sideways, their weapons drawn. The level of crazy astounded him. Pelter would take them all down. They'd given Pelter enough.

"You're under arrest, you'll surrender your weapons to Deputy Gramble, my men will handcuff you, read your rights—"

Thorpe snarled, "Fuck you, it's all their fucking faults. Bringing their lifestyles here. This was a decent town until all these fags and hippies took over. It was just fucking fine without that goddamned bitch." Thorpe had his weapon trained on Peaches.

He noticed it before anyone else, it was a microscopic movement but enough. Thorpe began to compress the trigger. Training took over, and he aimed—took a deep breath and squeezed. The shot struck Thorpe in the shoulder. Then everything went into slow motion and garbled.

The reverberation of simultaneous shots resounded through the night. A sledgehammer to sternum knocked him off his feet, a feminine scream rang out, joined by masculine ones. The pain in his chest dimmed his vision, but he saw Peaches on the ground. Blood blossoming in a macabre rose over the fabric at her shoulder. Cabot and Post were down, their pain-filled moans almost overshadowed the shouting of several of the Crews' calls for paramedics. Pelter and Linus stood side by side, weapons leveled at Thorpe.

The man wasn't going down, as he compressed his trigger again, Pelter and Linus returned fire. Thorpe stumbled back until he hit the front of his cruiser and the metal of the hood sounded as if it collapsed beneath his bulk.

He was gasping for breath as he rolled to his stomach and crawled to Peaches. Pelter rushed to check Thorpe and Linus fell to his knees beside Peaches. Gib had already torn her shirt open. Tears stained her pale face, and she hid against Gib's stomach. A bar towel appeared and was pressed to the profusely bleeding wound.

"Where are the paramedics," Scary bellowed.

"On their way, one of my men is a medic, he's getting his kit, and he'll be here in two minutes," Pelter answered.

"It's okay, just a flesh wound," Peaches attempted to joke, but it fell flat.

"You ever do that to me again, I will spank you, do you hear me, woman?"

"Don't threaten me with a good time."

Gib cupped Peaches' face his one hand and tipped her chin up until their eyes met. "I haven't been able to live without you for over thirty years, please, don't do that to me again."

"Promise."

Their lips trembled as they shared a kiss and tears shimmered in Gib's eyes.

"You okay, Wren," Linus asked.

He didn't have a chance to answer before Linus ripped his uniform shirt open and check the vest.

"I told you no damn heroics."

Again, he was stopped from answering as firm lips slammed down on his and hands fisted roughly in his hair. He tasted tears and didn't know if they were his or Linus'. Linus' thick, muscled arms wrapped around him and held him to the point he could barely breathe. Which was already inhibited by what he knew were at least a few bruised ribs.

"Thorpe," his voice croaked as he asked.

"Dead."

"What happens?"

"My surveillance team has video and audio, it was a clean shoot, along with the last of the information y'all's man sent me tonight, Thorpe was already looking to die in a cell. When the cops show, are y'all going to talk or get all closed-mouthed?"

"What's in it for us if we talk?" Scary appointed himself spokesman.

Linus was too busy checking him for any other wounds. He almost smiled at the frown on Linus' handsome face along with the deep creases between his thick brows. He'd learned that when Linus was really annoyed the lines were extra deep and that's exactly how they looked now.

"Interim Sheriff will be appointed, and it'll probably be the same bullshit, just different fucker. What assurances do we have that in a few months' time we're not right back at this point?"

"I can't."

"Then we don't have anything to say. We could've handled this ourselves. No one would've found his ass and to be honest, a majority of the town wouldn't have given a shit."

"Scary, you do know I'm a cop, right?"

"Still the same punk kid, though."

He kept forgetting the new information of Scary and Pelter being cousins. They really didn't like each other for whatever reason.

"It's not my fault my dad was an asshole."

"Can we save the family squabble for another time, when we don't have a bleeding Peaches waiting for medical attention." Elijah popped out from behind Scary. "They'll cooperate…" Everyone started to grumble. "To an extent. I won't have my men and the rest of my family in harm's way. You have the video, so you shouldn't need extensive information from us. Hunter is not to be implicated in this at all, and if he is, you'll do your best to—"

"Hunter was working in an official capacity at my request, and I cleared it with his P.O. this afternoon."

"You better not implicate my son in this shit, I'll sic—"

Everyone including Peaches chuckled, Gregory was highly protective of Hunter. Hunter loved having Gregory as a father-figure, someone who loved him unconditionally. He wondered if Hunter knew what he meant to Linus and him?

"Do you think Hunter knows we love him," Wren whispered the question.

"Actually…shit, he's been acting weird today. He wouldn't let me hold him, I thought it was because we had the kids in the house, ya know?"

"We need to have a talk with him."

"We do, but first let's get this shit taken care of and then we can go the fuck home to our man, and our temporary kids."

"Not too temporary. I filed paperwork for emergency custody for them to be placed with Linus today," Peaches said.

He shot a look at Peaches to find a man in tactical gear wrapping her shoulder.

"What's she talking about?"

"Oh well, um, fuck, you looked kinda cute holding the former parasite and Hunter seemed to like it—"

"It has a name, Linus."

"Moving on. So, Derrick only needs a place to stay until he heads off to college in the fall and—"

"You got us kids?"

"Yeah, well, they'd be mine because, ya know, I'm the most stable one in this relationship."

"Stable, what's wrong with me and Hunter?"

"Nothing's wrong with Hunter, he's perfect, it's more you, I mean, you're a cop, one of your worst qualities."

"You're like your mother, I'm not quitting my job."

"We'll see."

Sirens broke off the argument he knew was going to happen. They'd deal with it later after they got through with the questioning and hospital to get checked out. Then he realized something.

"You're not fucking wearing your vest," he yelled. Linus disappeared, his man had a death wish. They were going to have to take care of that because he wasn't going to deal with worrying about his man for the next fifty-fucking-years.

20 LINUS WASN'T TERRIFIED OF THE MINI-HUMAN!

Cartoons played in the background, and he moved around the kitchen getting a bowl of cereal ready for the former parasite's breakfast. He called the kid Craig when no one else was around. He liked busting his men's balls when they got all offended and reminded him Craig had a name. He wasn't a complete novice at this. He'd been in charge of Matty countless times since his nephew was born.

It was just the fact that he was going to be his kid. He didn't know how Peaches pushed through the emergency custody, but he had a feeling her visit with Thorpe's wife had something to do with it. The swiftness of the transfer of custody pissed him off. Who the hell gave up their kid that quickly?

He understood someone not being able to take care of the child or children they had due to a lot of fucked up shit, but over the time he'd investigated the Thorpes, he found the woman to be cold and calculated. Her fat bank account more important. His opinion of her hadn't changed after he'd spent more time with Derrick.

The boy reminded him of Hunter. Derrick shied away from affection or compliments. Derrick seemed shocked when they offered to help him with his homework. Sometimes he ate like someone would take the plate away from him. They hadn't commented on it because they didn't want to embarrass him.

Hunter and Derrick were off to Atlanta for the day to visit the University campus and get set up with a dorm room or whatever.

"Linus," Craig squealed.

He turned to find the kid making grabby hands at the bowl he was still holding.

Focus, Trenton, you got a kid to feed, he chided himself.

He grabbed the sippy cup of juice and made his way to the table. Craig was in a booster seat. He set the bowl, spoon, and cup in front of Craig. Just like Derrick, the kid devoured his food.

"Slow down, you're gonna make yourself sick."

He flopped down into the chair and picked up his coffee, he brought it to his mouth as he noticed Craig staring at it.

"Want a sip," he asked and started to hand it to Craig.

"Don't even think about it," Wren ordered from the door.

"What, I wasn't doing anything," he said with a smile.

Wren's hair was sticking up all over, and his eyes were still heavy with sleep. They'd had a rough week. Wren was on leave for a few weeks, and he knew the man was rethinking his position as a Deputy. He might give the man shit about his job, but he knew Wren loved what he did.

His man hadn't taken the kill shot, but he knew Wren felt guilty and questioned whether the situation could've been handled differently. Him and Peaches, even Pelter assured him that it ended with the only logical outcome. Thorpe reached the point of no return, knew his days as a free man were numbered. He didn't doubt the man was mentally unstable as well.

He grinned at Wren headed toward the coffeemaker, but made a b-line to him and leaned down to give him a slow, deep kiss.

"Kiss," there was another squeal.

Wren's lips curved into a smile against his, and then Wren straightened and turned to Craig. His man kissed Craig's soft, blond hair. Craig giggled then continued eating.

Craig and Derrick were fitting in around his house just like Hunter and Wren. He was dreading the day they felt it was time to head back to their own places. He knew it would happen. He couldn't keep them there forever. Part of him asked why not because Lily and Damon lived together pretty much since the day they met.

They weren't his parents, and not everything was a fairy tale like it appeared to be for Lily and Damon. He didn't remember his parents ever having a serious fight.

"What time are Hunter and Derrick due back," Wren asked as he poured himself a huge mug of coffee.

"I don't know, I think they said they were probably going to grab dinner before they headed back."

"So, they left you in charge of Craig?"

"Man, I've watched kids before, I ain't 'fraid of no mini-human."

"I didn't say you were."

"I can see you smiling, asshole."

"Asshole," Craig said with a giggle.

"Now, see what you did?"

"I didn't do anything, I can't help the former parasite was a parrot in a past life."

"I didn't think Atheists believed in past lives."

"Figure of speech. Don't be a dick." He shot a look at Craig and saw the boy's mouth opening, "Don't even think about saying it. Bad words."

Wren chuckled and turned to lean back against the counter.

He stood, removed Craig from the chair, and placed him in the pinned off area in the corner of the kitchen. The kid loved to play hide and seek, and the little shit was professional level. He'd already lost him twice. "No jail breaks. If you're anything like your new family, you better get used to small, confined spaces."

"Linus, don't say that to him," Wren admonished.

He strode slowly across the kitchen to Wren and plucked the mug from the man's hand, and he set it on the counter. He slipped his arms around Wren's waist and tugged the man closer. Wren's skin was smooth and warm against his.

"What are you doing," Wren asked as he draped his arms over his shoulders.

"I thought I was getting close to my man, but if you—"

A smirk pulled at the corner of his mouth as Wren rolled his eyes. He nudged Wren's chin with his nose until the man tipped his head back. He sucked at Wren's Adam's apple, nuzzled Wren's perfectly trimmed beard, and tongued the rapid pace of Wren's pulse.

"Fuck, you're sexy. I hated you the first time I saw you."

"Thanks," Wren asked sarcastically.

"You know what I mean."

"I saw you and Hunter together...I felt like an outsider."

"Do you still feel like an outsider?"

He wanted the answer to be no, he was amazed how Scary, Elijah, and Tank made it work. They'd spent time together, learned about each other, but it still didn't seem like enough. With the threat of Thorpe gone, it should've felt easier, yet it caused more complications. Then the fact he decided Derrick and Craig weren't going anywhere. They were his, and he could see how much Wren and Hunter had come to care for them. Maybe it was too fast, and he'd admit it, that didn't mean he wouldn't try to keep the five of them together as long as possible.

"No, I don't. I'm just..."

"Just what?"

Wren's lightly calloused hands came to rest on his chest and combed his fingers through the thick mat of hair.

He watched Wren's expression, he had become adept at sensing both his men's moods, but Wren kept his emotions a lot more in check than Hunter. The uncertainty Wren felt about the three of them caused him to feel helpless, and he didn't know how to reassure Wren.

"Everything just seemed to go to Hell. You were shot because you're a dumbass—"

"Hey, I knew what I was doing."

Wren snorted. "Your version of reality is majorly fucking skewed, but you're not distracting me. Thorpe and all his bullshit, the shooting. I'm lost on what to do."

Wren dropped his forehead to his shoulder, and he lifted his hand to massage the back of Wren's neck.

"What you're going to do is take your leave. Spend some time with us. All that other shit will work itself out."

"What am I going to do for work?"

"If you don't want to go back to the Sheriff's department, then come to work for me."

"Really?"

"Yeah, and what do you mean really?"

"Have you met your own crew?"

"They're a little...eccentric." He barely said that with a straight face. His guys became family over the short years they'd worked together. He'd recruited them from everywhere. Their pasts not his to reveal, a few of them survived the worst humanity could throw at them. He welcomed them with every quirk, big or small. They had his back, and he'd always have theirs.

"That title is usually reserved for reclusive billionaires and doesn't Little live in his van?"

"He doesn't live in his van, but we're not exactly sure where he does live. He suffers from paranoia. You want a lecture on every conspiracy theory ever, then he's the man to talk to."

"Why doesn't that surprise me?"

Wren's husky laugh seemed to lighten the heavy stress which weighted Wren down.

"There's the smile I've been looking for." He brushed his lips to the corners of Wren's mouth.

He pressed his body fully to Wren. The man was hard and muscled, only slightly shorter than him. He loved the contrast between his men, but they were both sweet and loving, the softness he needed.

"I don't want you and Hunter to leave."

"We've been living here for almost two months. Hell, we've moved in half our shit."

"I know it ain't going to be easy. Couples like my parents, and Peaches and Gib, are exceptions to the rule, but I can't imagine not coming home and you two not being here."

"Shouldn't we have this conversation with Hunter?"

"He's pulling away."

"I don't think it's so much he's pulling away as he's unsure of how we feel."

"What do you mean unsure, I love him, have for a long time. He should—"

"Linus, our man is a bit insecure, I'm sure you've noticed that."

"But we compliment him. Touch him. Show him we care."

"But have we told him?"

"Fuck, and we still haven't sat down and talked."

"Why don't we see if Lily would like some Grandma time with Craig and Derrick? A night of just the three of us before it's the five of us full-time."

"I'll give her a call. Watch the heathen?"

"I think I got the newest inmate covered."

"Good." He kissed Wren roughly, then stepped to the side and poured Wren a fresh cup of coffee. "I'll see if Ma would watch Matty too."

"Please have a conversation about appropriate behavior around our kids."

He nearly lost it at the thought of anything being appropriate when it came to his mother. He didn't bother answering and left Wren warning Craig about spending time with his new grandmother.

Lily would jump at the chance to spend time with her grandchildren. She'd waited a long time. He wanted alone time with his men to make his and Wren's intention clear to Hunter. He hadn't made the best impression on Hunter, and he'd never masked his aversion to monogamy.

He needed Wren and Hunter to understand they were it for him. They were everything he had wanted but was afraid to hope for. Okay, the two boyfriends' thing was a bit of a shocker, yet it felt perfect and right. He entered his office and grabbed his phone from his desk. First, get his mother to watch the newest Trentons, and plan a date with his men, then make sure his new family stuck together.

21 HE WASN'T A COMPLETE FUCK UP?

Smoke filled the kitchen and Hunter snapped a towel at the blaring smoke alarm. He had the doors and windows open while smoke billowed from the oven. All he had to do was heat it up per Twitch's instructions. Turn on the oven. Heat. That was it and what did he do, turned it into a lump of charcoal. At least his fingertips were only minimally singed and barely hurt.

Wren and Linus said they were going to take him on a date. He didn't want to go out, he only wanted to spend time with them, and thought cooking a frozen fucking dinner would be safe. Wren went to drop the kids off with Lily, and Linus was headed home from the office.

Linus had some kind of meeting with Pelter.

The alarm finally ceased. His nose and throat burned, so he walked backward until he fell into one of the kitchen chairs. He rested his elbows on his knees and buried his face in his hands. Tears dampened his cheeks. Why couldn't he do something as simple as making dinner without fucking it up?

Linus and Wren were capable. Gorgeous. Successful. And there he was sitting in a smoky kitchen with tears streaming down his cheeks forming pools in the cups of his palms.

"Hunter," Wren and Linus called his name in panicked tones.

He didn't bother looking up as pounding steps signaled their progress until the sound stopped.

"Hey," Wren said, then Wren's strong hands circled his wrists.

He sobbed as he fought Wren's hold.

"Are you burned, let us see," Linus ordered.

"I'm fine."

"Then what's wrong?"

"I burned dinner."

"And," Wren asked. "Baby, it's not like we can't make something else or go out to eat."

"But I wanted to make dinner and just hang—"

"Hunter, look at us, now," Linus' voice carried a hardened edge.

He lifted his head to find them crouched down in front of him and watching him, but he didn't see any recrimination.

Linus had a hand on his right thigh and Wren on his left. Their thumbs tenderly stroking in soothing passes.

"It's burned dinner, anyone can do it, hell, I don't even cook. I'm sure I can say this for Linus and me, we appreciate you wanting to make us dinner. Why we love you has nothing to do with whether you can microwave dinner or cook a five-course gourmet meal. You're sweet. Caring. Intelligent. You're so many things."

They both leaned in, their lips brushed his cheeks to the corners of his mouth. His men wrapped him in their arms and held him tight. Wren's words repeatedly played in his head, but one word, in particular, caused his heart to pick up painfully in his chest. Love. He'd never received love outside his chosen family. Gregory was free with his declarations and positive reinforcement, but that wasn't romantic love.

This, Wren and Linus, this was so much more than he'd ever allowed himself to hope for, but he couldn't voice the word—the questions.

"We have frozen pizza and all the soda you can drink, we can all work together."

"I'd...I'd like that."

"But first, we have some things to talk about." Linus plopped down onto the floor, and Wren followed.

Their poses perfectly mirrored, their forearms rested on their raised knees.

"Wren and me talked, and we think we've fucked up."

"No, no, you—"

"We should've sat down and had this conversation weeks ago," Wren said.

"What conversation," he asked. His stomach twisted into knots.

Linus and Wren shared a look before they turned back to him.

Linus sighed softly. "We talked and realized we haven't told you how we feel about you. Maybe we thought we showed you."

"We love you, everything about you. Even the things you see as faults."

"You're fucking beautiful to us. I ain't no prize, and you'd probably be better off with Wren, but I won't give you up. We won't give you up. I don't want y'all to leave. I want you two in my house…my bed for as long as I can keep y'all."

He drew his brows together. Linus had a bit of a fatalist attitude with a glass half empty philosophy. Did Linus believe he wanted to be anywhere else?

"I love being here. I love the two of you. What if I'm more trouble than I'm worth?"

"Hunter, to us you could never be trouble or a bother." Wren smiled at him, then leaned into Linus. "We know this won't be easy. But I can speak for myself, I can't imagine being anywhere else. So, this is it for us, Linus and me talked, and we realized you were starting to pull away. We'd like to know why or what we did to make you—"

"Linus said the other night that I was sweet and caring, two of the reasons he loved me. I thought…I don't know, I thought maybe it was just a figure of speech."

Linus rolled to his knees and knelt between his thighs, then Linus' hands cupped his cheeks.

"It wasn't a fucking figure of speech. This shit is new to me, baby, I don't know anything about relationships, but I'm positive that I love you and Wren."

He studied Linus' handsome face, the way his oddly colored eyes shone with a familiar emotion. One he'd seen countless times aimed in his direction when Linus watched him. All the times Linus leaned in to gently kiss his forehead.

He glanced at Wren to find a similar warmth in Wren's gaze. As his shoulders relaxed, he hadn't realized how stiffly he had held himself.

"Hunter, we want to hear what you want," Wren spoke as he came to kneel on his right side.

"I want to stay here with you two."

"And?"

"Our kids."

"Yeah, I kinda turned myself into a package deal with the former parasites. One's moving out soon though."

"I don't mind, Craig and Derrick need us."

"They do, and they are staying right here." Wren stood.

The man grabbed his hand and Linus', tugging them to their feet.

He had a family. One who loved and needed him, a family he wouldn't have to worry about losing when he wasn't good enough because to Linus and Wren he was— perfect even in his imperfection.

They hugged each other around their waists and shared kisses, touches. His men's hard dicks pushed to his hips. His breathing picked up as Linus pulled Wren and him from the kitchen, down the hall and into their bedroom.

In silent agreement, they separated only long enough to remove their clothing. Wren and Linus were similarly built, broad and muscled, where Wren's stomach was deeply grooved Linus' had a firm curve covered in a thick mat of hair. He was soft, his stomach rounded and his thighs fleshy, but his men looked at him like he was everything they had ever wanted.

They came together sharing kisses and touches. Their hard cocks bumped. They shifted until Wren became sandwiched between them. Linus held them tight, and Wren leaned his head back on Linus' shoulder.

He took a step away, Linus and Wren watched him as Linus stroked his hands over Wren's stomach up to pinch at Wren's flat pebbled nipples. They were sexy together.

Smooth against hairy, dark to light, and scarred to flawless. They never took their eyes from him.

He caressed his hand down his stomach and then lower to circle his cock. He stroked his cock in slow, firm strokes, and he plucked at his nipples.

"I think our man wants your ass, you gonna give it to him, Wren?" Linus bit and sucked at Wren's pulse.

Wren jerkily nodded as he arched and pushed his ass against Linus.

"Baby, get our man ready," Linus ordered.

He swallowed as he released his dick and walked to the low nightstand and opened the drawer. He pulled two condoms and the lube out, he turned, and his breath caught as he found Wren bent at the waist, his fists planted on the mattress as Linus knelt behind him, his face buried between Wren's muscled cheeks. Sweat beaded on Wren's face and his eyes were clenched shut.

Wren gruffly cursed as he rocked his hips backward. His whole body clenched as Linus brought his hands down on Wren's ass, one cheek then the other. He closed the distance between him and the bed. Linus sat back on his heels, and he looked down at Wren's spit slicked hole.

He dropped the condoms to the mattress. He used his thumb to flip open the cap, squeezed it onto his fingers, and brought them to Wren's crease. Standing to the side to let Linus watch, he massaged the wrinkled skin and felt it clench under his fingertips. Linus kneaded Wren's hard, thick thighs as he quickly worked his fingers into Wren. The skin silky and hot, contracting around the digits. He quickly added fingers until he fucked Wren with four.

Wren begged and whimpered while his body slick with sweat and his dark hair stuck to his face and neck. His man's face flushed. He turned his attention to Linus to find the man focused on them, his chest lifted and fell with his labored breaths.

"Lay down on the bed," Linus' voice barely more than a growl. "Put on the condom."

He did as ordered, and he shifted until his head rested on the pillows. Wren's eyes were glittering slits, and Wren shook violently.

Linus held onto Wren's hips and assisted him onto the bed to straddle his hips. Wren's thighs and calves were hot against his skin. He had never wanted anyone as much as he did Linus and Wren.

Wren's arm moved behind him to hold his cock and Wren sank down onto his length. He clenched his teeth as he tried to hold it together. He inhaled the combined scents of his men. Wren rode him in a rough, erratic pace as Wren jacked his cock. The man looked beautiful and wild, uncontrolled.

He lifted his arm and curved his hand around the back of Wren's neck pulling the man down. He roughly kissed Wren, tongue-fucked Wren as he lifted and fell on his dick. The whines and grunts blended with the slap of sweaty skin, their bodies easily slid together. It was a flawless dance as he lifted his hips to match Wren's.

He opened his eyes to find Linus behind Wren. Linus' gaze fixed on where his dick stroked into Wren's tight hole.

"Wren, baby, do you think you can take me," Linus asked as he draped his broad body over Wren's back.

Wren's mouth fell open, Wren and him arched into each other as he felt the smooth length of Linus' cock stroke against his.

"Be still, baby, fuck, s'sexy, fucking per…"

He watched Linus' eyes close, and his lids fell as Linus slipped into Wren. Wren's fingers clenched in his hair, and

Wren's free arm came up and back to twine around Linus' neck.

"You okay," Linus asked Wren.

Linus tenderly lavished Wren's neck and shoulder with light brushes.

"Y—yes. Please, more."

It became a seamless dance, they thrust and retreated in tandem as they loved their man. They both whispered to Wren of their love, how he was theirs. Quick panicked groans preceded a long, harsh moan as wet heat spread between Wren and his belly. They rode their man through his orgasm, pushed through the rhythmic tightening. He shouted as he lost control and spilled into the condom, Linus' own sound of completion echoed through the room. Linus collapsed onto Wren, crushing the man between them.

He wrapped his arms around Wren and Linus, stroking hot skin. He groaned as Wren and Linus slid to the side, they gathered each other close as their breathing calmed. He didn't feel a need to speak as he shared kisses and touches with his men. Felt loved and needed, it was his secret dream come true. They whispered their love as tears leaked from the corners of his eyes, and even as he attempted to hide it, Wren and Linus brushed the tears away with kisses, and he accepted the affection, savored it and knew he would never have to give it up.

22 THERE'S A NEW SHERIFF IN TOWN

Coarse hair abraded his back, and Wren's fingers fisted around the edge of the sink. He could barely brace himself against the powerful thrust of Linus' hips. Sweaty skin slapped together almost overshadowed by their combined grunts.

"Open your eyes," Linus ordered.

He opened his eyes to meet Linus' gaze in the mirror. Linus' cheeks were flushed, and long lashes fanned Linus' cheeks. Linus straightened, and his rough hands curled over his shoulders.

He started to drop his chin only to earn a growl from Linus.

"Don't fucking look away."

He lifted his leg to rest his knee on the sink and opened himself more, to take Linus deeper. He was so fucking close, Linus' dick tortured his prostate, and then his eyes rolled back, and he came against the cabinets.

Linus powered into him one last time and froze, Linus' fat cock jerking inside him.

Muscles he'd held tensely relaxed as he laid his forehead on the mirror. His breath fogging the glass. He was never going to be able to make it to work. He chuckled and groaned as Linus bit between his shoulder blades.

"What's so funny," Linus asked.

"I don't want to go to work now."

"Is that a complaint?"

"Never, I would never complain about one of my men loving on me. You two do it a lot."

"I think that's mutual. I'll clean up your mess while you take a shower."

"That mess is all your fault." He shuddered as Linus pulled from him and then helped him stand. "I was getting ready for work when you decided—"

"I'm so feeling the complaints."

"Shut up." Wren pushed a kiss to Linus' mouth and restarted the shower. He stepped under the scalding spray and quickly washed.

He noticed Linus cleaning up the cabinet then himself before getting dressed in pajama bottoms and leaving the bathroom.

A lot changed in the last three months. He'd met and fell in love with two men, nearly lost his job, moved in with his boyfriends and now co-parent to Derrick and Craig. That wasn't where he'd seen himself when he'd moved to Powers.

Today a new chapter started, he finished showering and then jumped out, drying off quickly. He was already late, so he rushed into the bedroom and dressed in his uniform. Their interim Sheriff became permanent today. He was not looking forward to working with the man. It was definitely going to be a challenge, especially with who he dated.

He jogged into the kitchen, accepted the to-go mug of coffee from Hunter while the taller man bounced Craig on his hip. Linus was helping Derrick with his homework. Thorpe's wife had signed over full custody and her rights a few weeks before making the boys theirs.

Shit, his phone started ringing, and he was sure it was his new boss.

"I gotta go, love y'all." he said as he kissed and hugged everyone bye, running from the house.

■■■

"Gramble, what time does your shift start?"

He concealed his eye roll and then turned to look at Sheriff Pelter. The large man looked weird in a Sheriff's uniform and not in black tactical gear. The town council had unanimously hired Pelter on as the new Sheriff.

It had made sense, the man was a heart attack waiting to happen, and he'd needed a change of pace.

"Sorry, I overslept," he grimaced. Lying wasn't allowed in their house, but he wasn't at home.

"Whatever you say, Gramble, make sure it doesn't happen again.

"Yes, sir." He strolled to his desk, bent over to open his bottom drawer and stowed his backpack.

"I need to talk to you about something." Pelter pulled up a chair and sat down. The man raised his hands and scrubbed his palms over his face.

"What is it?"

"I've been going over all the reports, what concerns me is what isn't in them."

"Like what?"

"Hate crimes, domestic violence, I got a ton of drunk and disorderly, petty theft, but…I heard rumors about a series of attacks on one resident in particular."

"Harper. She's a sweetheart. A little skittish and keeps to herself."

"I checked hospital reports, she's been in the ER multiple times in the last few years and not one report or investigation. Hospital policy in such cases is to contact law enforcement and report it."

He knew where this was going. It wasn't like he hadn't wanted to investigate the incidents, but without Harper's cooperation, there was nothing he could do.

"Unless Harper talks we don't have anything to go on. Everyone knows around here, yeah, Bill gets away with beating the shit out of Harper to hide the fact they may possibly be having a sexual relationship. I don't doubt it's nonconsensual. She keeps her head down, her mouth shut and…"

He hated what Harper was going through. She was a sweet woman. Went out of her way for those she cared about, but no matter how many times they tried to draw her out of her shell, she retreated.

"This I know, but all this stops now. We're not going to look the other way."

"Definitely not. I'll make sure to keep an extra eye on Harper. Joker knows every time she's gone to the ER, call him in and he can give you all the details you want."

"Do you think he'll talk to me?"

"Yeah, but don't come up behind him. Don't touch him. And whatever you do, don't corner him. Badge or not, the man will take you down."

"I've seen his sheet. He's a regular guest."

Wren had seen the same file, Joker couldn't be considered anything but a vigilante. A woman gets knocked around by her husband or boyfriend, the bastard conveniently ended up with a broken bone or two. A gay couple gets harassed, and it never happened again. With the man's past, the abuse the man suffered it surprised him Joker used his rage for good.

"He's good, Sheriff."

"I'm going to trust you on that, but things are going to change in this town. I won't put up with Thorpe's ghosts, do we understand each other?"

"Crystal clear."

Pelter didn't say anything else, just stood and headed for his office. Wren slumped back in his chair and scrubbed his hand over his short beard. Pelter was on a mission, with the skeleton crew they were running on it was going to make his life even more difficult, but that didn't matter. When he left work at the end of his shift, he had his family to go home to, and that was all that mattered to him.

He reopened his drawer, slid the zipper on his back open and reached in for the frame he'd put there last night. This was where everything changed, he placed the picture on his desk and smiled as he looked at it. He'd never had anyone special enough to put on his desk, now, he had four.

Twitch had taken the picture for him last weekend, he and Linus stood on either side of Hunter. The big man held Craig to his chest and Derrick was in front of them, they'd hugged the awkward and sullen teenager as they'd taken their first family photo. He didn't have to hide anymore, Powers was the place he'd found home and a place to belong, men he loved. It was almost perfect, and almost perfect was damn fine with him.

ABOUT THE AUTHOR

By day, J.M. is an introverted cook hiding out in her kitchen in the middle of nowhere Ohio, by night and any free time she may have, she is a writer of mainly LGBTQ Fiction and Erotica. Although. she's equal opportunity when it comes to telling a story, she'll even write a bit of straight erotic romance when the mood strikes.

She has been writing for years in old notebooks. At the age of eight, she wrote the worst poem in the history of poetry, but it sparked her love for writing. She reads too much and loves to get lost in other worlds and her favorite stories have to include laughter and having the reader doing at least one double take. Thirty-something, forever restless she uses her stories to ground herself, and find her place of peace.

WHERE TO FIND J.M.
www.jmdabneyauthor.com

www.ingramcontent.com/pod-product-compliance
Lightning Source LLC
Chambersburg PA
CBHW060152130626
46556CB00006B/2600